Heaven's Sacrifice

By

Scarlet Hunter

Dedication

To my uncle Joe who left us too soon.

I know he is amongst the angels in Heaven,
looking down on us all.

Acknowledgments

This book certainly would not have been published without the help of some very *special* people. LaVerne Thompson–I am blessed to have you in my life. I grow as a writer and person every day because of you. To my editors—thank you both—for this publication would not be possible.

Heaven's Sacrifice by Scarlet Hunter
Lucky Cl✳ver™ Publishing
Cordova, TN 38016
(The clover emblem/logo and the seal containing name Lucky Clover is a trademark of Lucky Cl✳ver™ Publishing)

First Edition Copyright© 2014
ISBN: 978-0-9884676-1-3

Lucky Cl ✳ver™ Publishing

Cover artist: Fiona Jayde
Editor: Faith Bicknell-Brown and Leanore Elliott

Lucky Cl✤ver™ Publishing

Warning: **This book may contain graphic sexual material and/or profanity and is not meant to be read by any person under the age of 18.**

Prologue

Beyond the starry twilight, Heaven's realm glimmered. A kingdom existing high above countless worlds in the solar system, consisting of immortal creatures of a variety of species, many undiscovered. While some planets remained unexplored, God kept a keen watch over one particular planet— Earth. A prosperous and energetic world inhabited by mortal humans. Ordained by God Himself, they were given one chance at life. With that fact known among the race, there were those who took it for granted. Some tried their best at merely surviving it, but little did they know such temperaments toward this way of life would draw a fine line for their existence.

Over the years, the human population increased. More and more mortal minds and souls were corrupted by sin. The vast work of Satan lurked and steered the weak-minded into directions not of righteousness, but of hate and deceit.

It was the very reason God appointed His sanctioned angels to venture down and help those in need. But at a cost. If they failed the task, the angels would lose their most prized possession treasured above all—their wings. A risk looked upon as a virtuous sacrifice. All for the sake of humans, in the hopes they could rekindle the good they once beheld...

Chapter One

"Now, I *know* he's not comin' up in here lookin' like that!"

"Girl, please. Be nice." Ava elbowed Brianna on the arm.

Ava and her sister, Brianna, stood behind the front counter, both staring out the window of their office building. The beauty of the ocean shoreline made it a splendid vacation spot. Although, for the past couple of years, visitors preferred Myrtle Beach, making it a more popular place for beachgoers.

For five successful years, they had worked for a family-owned condo resort in Kure Beach, North Carolina. The oceanfront units were located fifteen miles south of Wilmington.

"Look at what he's wearin'. If he's here for the interview, don't even think about hirin' him," Brianna continued.

Of the two, she voiced an unmistakable southern accent. Ava did too, but not nearly as strong as her sister's.

"Shhh. Stop it, Brie. If he is, you know how badly we need someone who can be useful around here. I'm just too busy." Ava turned her gaze to Brianna and arched an eyebrow. "Unless, *you* want to fix and re-stain the wood siding, repair missing planks from the catwalk, as well as be on call twenty-four hours a day for maintenance. I fixed the toilet in the Sea Breeze unit yesterday, and I still don't think the damn thing flushes right."

Brianna rolled her eyes, and flashed her fresh set of French manicured nails out in front of her. "Whatever, and ruin these nails. Are you crazy?"

"Like I said, we *need* someone. Look." Ava slid a piece of paper in front of Brianna. "If this guy is here for the job, he is more than qualified. Did you read this?"

Her sister glanced down, but didn't make an effort to read it, only admiring her painted nails she held out in front of her.

"I talked to Uncle DeWayne this morning. He's going to be out for months, probably the whole summer. We need to hire someone who can take on his responsibilities that I'm unable to do."

Brianna huffed and flung her arms up in the air. "Yeah, well when he steals all the flat-screens, it will be YOU callin' DeWayne on his deathbed tellin' him he might as well have God take 'im cuz his business is up in smoke."

Recently their uncle DeWayne had been suddenly struck down with a serious illness. Doctors predicted he would be hospitalized for months for observation and treatment. He called Ava when they admitted him and broke the bad news, hoping the two girls could hold down the fort and handle business without him.

"BRIANNA!" Ava snapped.

"What? I'm just sayin'. Don't come to me when it happens. I'll just say I told you so."

Ava drew a deep breath and released it sharply. "You really are something, you know that?" she said, shaking her head. There were times she wanted to strangle her sister, but somehow always held her composure.

"Fine. Whatever. I'm out. You handle this on your own." Brianna snorted and stormed out through the side entrance. As always, she'd left the business decisions up to Ava. No doubt Brianna headed in the direction she normally went each day at this time—the beach. Not caring that she was still on the clock.

Ava released a sigh and her thoughts immediately went to her uncle. A longtime widower, after his wife passed away from cancer many years ago, his only income came from his remaining asset—the condos.

Five years ago, when Ava was seventeen and Brianna fourteen, DeWayne always felt he needed to do everything to support and take care of them. Ava could have gone off to college, but DeWayne needed her and there was no way she could keep her grades up and handle everything with the business.

So, she put her dreams aside, and did what was necessary for her uncle.

However, his recent illness couldn't have come at a worse time for him, and Ava couldn't let DeWayne down. It'd been a Tuesday afternoon when DeWayne called her at the office. His normal monthly check-up ended with him being admitted to the hospital. While Ava helped Betsy, their only maid, fold towels in the laundry room across from the office, the cordless phone resting on top the dryer rang.

"Kure Beach Resorts, may I help you?" Ava said warmly.

"Ava. It's me."

"What's wrong?" she asked, worried. She could tell by his voice something wasn't right.

"I'm fine. Some of my tests came back and the doctor wants to send me to the hospital…"

"What?" Ava yelled into the receiver.

"Don't worry. They just want to run some tests. They have more advanced machines at the hospital. I'm heading there now, but I'm afraid it will take some time. They want to admit me."

"Oh, Uncle," Ava paused, not knowing what to say. "What did the doctor's tell you? Why are they admitting you?"

"It's my kidneys again. The levels are worse than before and the doctors are concerned."

"I'm on my way." Ava never let on to him how concerned she felt. With DeWayne dealing with health issues for a little over a year, the news didn't come as a total shock. But he'd been doing so well, up till now. Or so, she'd thought. After she hung up, she sank further into the office chair, threw her elbows on his desk, covered her face in her hands and wept. Uncertain if she could pull off a miracle, but prayed for one that very night.

Once she got to the hospital, she tried calming him and told him not to worry and to just focus on getting well. She assured him the business would be fine. The truth of the matter was, business had already been slow. But now, with him in the hospital, would she be able to manage the place alone? She'd have to master everything and who would handle the maintenance for the units?

Of course, breaking the news to Brianna went as expected. She didn't even go with Ava to the hospital. Her sister just ranted and raved, making sure she'd continue to get the same pay and pointed out *she* would not be taking on more responsibilities.

"It's not my problem!" Ava recalled her saying. Oh, how that girl needed a good kick in the ass.

Chapter Two

*A*va blinked a few times, shaking off her worries and focused on the man as he made his way up the catwalk. His jeans, covered with holes, appeared to be from wear and tear, not fashion. The main reason why her sister gave him no attention. From a distance, his shirt looked like it used to be white, yet now sported more of a bluish-gray tint. It looked torn at the bottom and the sleeves were ripped, obviously by choice, as strings of fabric ringed his huge upper biceps. Though, Ava couldn't deny the stranger seemed charming, despite the way he dressed.

From where she stood, he walked like a confident, interesting man. One who also happened to be their only source of help. After a few dozen phone calls, he was the only one who fit the qualifications listed in the ad Ava took out in the local newspaper. Plus, the sound of his voice made her strangely weak in the knees. When they spoke yesterday, it was a conversation she wouldn't ever forget.

"Are you the lady I need to speak with about the maintenance position?" A deep, solid and sturdy tone vibrated from the other end of the line.

"Yes."

"I'm calling to apply, if it is still available."

"Yes, yes it is," Ava replied. Just the manner of his voice made her heart rate increase with each syllable.

"Let me know when it is convenient for you and I can stop by."

For some reason she couldn't speak. A few short pauses and finally she answered, "Um, sure. How about tomorrow, say seven in the evening? Is that too late for you?"

"Perfect. I will see you tomorrow. And your name is…?"

"Oh yeah, sorry—Ava."

"I look forward to meeting you, Ava." Then the receiver went dead.

She held the phone to her ear with sweaty palms until the loud dial tone pierced her hearing. She smiled and slowly hung up the phone. Of course, expressing her interests to Brianna would only ignite her sister's competitive nature, so she kept her thoughts about the man to herself.

Materializing on earth, Percival appeared and stood on the sand, next to a long worn-out catwalk. He scanned the countless planks of rotten wood. They undoubtedly needed some TLC in more ways than one. By the looks of the property surrounding it, the newspaper ad was spot on. A skilled handyman was needed for this kind of job.

For a moment, he savored the calming, therapeutic waves crashing on shore. The sound felt like an explosion of love over the soul. Percival prayed with thanks, glad his mission had brought him near the Atlantic Ocean.

Lifting his foot, he placed it on the edge of the catwalk and putting some weight on it, wiggled his leg a few times on the board to ensure it would hold him. Convinced it would, he placed his full weight on the plank and noticed the whole length of the catwalk was covered with pieces of slivered wood, poking out from its depleted state. Thankful his sandals protected his feet, he proceeded toward the building.

In the heavens and before leaving, the angels were normally briefed about their assignments. Yet, Percival wasn't given specifics for his mission. He certainly would not question the lack of information, because in Heaven, one never asked questions but is grateful for the facts received. If God thought angels needed to know more, he made sure they did.

Everything has a purpose.

When he advanced, he inspected the building. Percival could tell it'd been constructed of the same wood as the catwalk and in the same dire need of attention. As his gaze skimmed up and across its surface, he imagined the structure probably appeared very elegant back in its day, yet now seemed in disrepair.

Unexpectedly, a squeal came from behind him, catching him off guard. Percival turned to find a small boy pointing at him while tugging at his father's swim shorts. Funny, how he hadn't even noticed them when he arrived. He needed to be more careful and assess his surroundings first.

"Look Pa. That man has wings!"

Oops, forgot about you two back there. Percival willed his thick, colossal set of feathery, white wings to fade from the mortal eye. He then nodded at the father and winked at the boy, who now displayed a saddened expression.

"I swear, Pa, he did—just like the Archangel."

The father took the boy by the hand and led him toward their car. "Not everyone is a comic book character, son. C'mon, let's go home."

Relieved his carelessness didn't require him to handle the situation further, Percival watched the two leave.

The boy's face remained glued to the passenger window of the SUV until they were out of sight. No doubt, waiting and hoping for the set of wings to reappear.

Cracking a smile at how he loved the Children of God, Percival returned his attention to his task. He reached into the front pocket of his jeans. After pulling out a piece of torn paper, he glanced at the newspaper ad, then at the building. Confirming the numbers 882 barely hanging above the door's entrance, he double-checked the name Ava, he'd written under the job qualifications. When she answered his call, the sound of her voice sang like church bells. Soft and angelic, it carried the slightest hint of a twang he'd never heard before. He sensed right off, she was unique by the way she spoke to him. Percival liked her instantly and looked forward to meeting her.

With his pull on the front door, a squeak wailed from the hinges. He cringed as he entered. His first impression of the place forced one word into his mind–old. He needed to fix this right away. The feeling of staying at a run-down hole-in-the-wall wouldn't make a good impression on guests when they arrived. He would bet the owners didn't even have the needed supplies to get the place in shipshape order. He'd take care of that too.

While Percival made his way farther into the small front area, a tall, slender woman stood up behind a counter centered directly along a bright teal wall covered with seashells and other kinds of beach artifacts. Trying his best to observe what else required immediate attention, his gaze kept returning to the attractive woman. He'd heard from other angels how before they left Heaven, they were able to view their human assignment. Having taken in this woman's beauty, it didn't matter now about not getting a first glance from Heaven. Then, a strange feeling at not wanting to share her with anyone flashed through his mind. His shielded wings started tingling. Jealousy flooded him. *What a peculiar reaction.*

Shaking off the unfamiliar sensation, he closed the last several feet separating him and the woman. He grinned before placing his forearm on the glass-top counter. A quick glance down, showed him a display of post cards, souvenirs and pictures. He didn't quite focus on them, because the woman drew his attention. She blessed him with a warm smile and it took his breath away.

After clearing his throat, he flashed his perfect set of angel-white teeth, returning the smile as he spoke, "I am here to see Ava. My name is Paul."

Chapter Three

As Ava stared through the front window, the man's character, aside from his clothing, presented a firm frame. When the door opened and he walked in, she hoped he would be the answer to her prayers.

In walked an extremely tall body of steel. A man of force.

When he proceeded closer, she caught sight of his tan skin. Apparently, he spent his days in the sun.

Ava tried not to appear too obvious, keeping her gaze on the paperwork, but couldn't help it as her gaze on its own accord drifted back to him. A handsome face, remarkably clean shaven, thick, dark-brown hair cut short around his neckline. The moment he stopped and placed his arm on the edge of the front desk, he smiled with the most perfect set of pearly white teeth she'd ever seen.

Wow. He would be ideal for a toothpaste commercial.

What really drew her attention was his striking eyes. She'd never seen such a mesmerizing color. Deep golden-yellow, outlined in a bright shade of green. They reminded her of apricots. The longer she gazed into them, the more her body temperature rose. The clearing of his throat and sound of his voice when he said his name broke her from her trance.

Ava blinked, and heat rushed to her face.

Paul? He sure doesn't look like a Paul. More along the lines of Hank the Hunk.

She giggled on the inside and opened her mouth to speak, but nothing came out. Clearing her throat, she grew more flustered and finally managed to say, "I'm Ava."

Just then, a side door swung open and Brianna strutted in, wearing nothing but an electric-purple bikini.

Ava rolled her eyes. *Freaking brilliant!*

Unfolding and shaking out a hot-pink and white striped beach towel, Brianna bent over to drape it across a bright-blue lounge chair. In frustration, she turned and tilted a blue umbrella this way and that, trying to keep it from casting a shadow over her chair.

"Can I help you there, sweetheart?" a man said from behind her.

Brianna peeped over her shoulder and found two guys admiring the scenery.

One stood with his hands inside his black swim short pockets, and the other closest to her grinned as he placed both hands at the sides of his v-shaped hips.

Brianna smiled and dreamingly skimmed both men's bodies. They were both cute, but the one without a shirt caught her attention. Standing up straight, she played with her blonde locks of hair. "Sure."

The one with black swim-shorts remained still while the shirtless guy walked past her and took the umbrella from her grasp.

"What's your name?" he asked.

"Brianna."

"I'm Marc. And that's—" The guy pointed at the other man.

"I'm not interested in him," Brianna cut him off while licking her lips and twirling hair around her fingertips.

The guy smirked. "Well then, how about you and I have some fun?" He wiggled his bleach-blonde eyebrows.

Brianna's grin grew, knowing exactly what he meant by 'fun' and was totally on board. She stopped playing with her hair and traced designs up and down the guy's tanned chest then softly circling her finger around one nipple. "You'll have to ditch your friend." She jerked her head in the other guy's direction.

The guy winked and took her by the waist. "Don't worry your pretty little head about him." A good six inches taller than her, Marc leaned in and whispered, "We can have a little party, just the two of us. How does that sound?" At the same time, he pointed at one of the condos behind them. It appeared he stayed at the resort next to theirs.

"I'm all for that, sexy," she replied, accepting the guy's proposal. At the same time, something caught her attention from the corner of her eye.

Well helllooo.

Through the side glass window of the office building, she caught a better view of the man who she'd paid no attention to earlier. The one she teased her sister about turned out to be more handsome than Brianna first thought.

Daaamn, I should have stuck around.

She couldn't tear her eyes away from him. Although he wore rags, it was nothing an introduction to *Abercrombie and Fitch* wouldn't fix, but the guy definitely had potential. She loved projects, especially when it came to the opposite sex, and there's no way she'd let Ava get to him before she got the chance to snatch him.

Quickly pulling away from Marc's grip, Brianna ran over to her chair. She grabbed her beach towel and tote filled with suntan lotions, sunglasses and cosmetics. Then, headed for the office building, yelling back, "Another time, big boy!"

On her way, a man with his wife and two young daughters holding cash approached her. "Excuse me, miss. I know you work at the condo here, so could you tell us how we can purchase lounge chairs and an umbrella?"

Brianna waved him off. "Not now, I'm busy." She kept walking. When she reached the building, she tossed her tote against the wall outside the door. She bent over and flipped her head forward to give her hair a good fluff. Throwing her head back, her long sandy-blonde locks fell freely along her shoulders and back. With her best seductive smile, she purposely left the beach towel behind and swung open the side door marked *Staff Only*.

The moment Brianna strutted in and stopped beside Mr. Eye Candy himself, she held her hand out in greeting. "Hello. I'm Brianna. Sorry I'm late. You must be here for the maintenance interview." She grinned, not once looking in Ava's direction. "Thank you for greeting him, Ava. I have this now. Sir, if you could kindly follow me." A sly smile crept over her lips as she again, strutted past the man. Sneaking a peek over

her shoulder to ensure his eyes were on her,
or rather her backside, she sent him her
sinful man-luring smile. "This way, please."

Chapter Four

*A*t the bite of her tongue, Ava did her best to compose herself, when in reality, she wanted to strangle Brianna. Not from jealousy. No, it's the inexcusable way she represented *Kure Beachfront Condominiums*. She couldn't stand it when Brianna acted this way. If DeWayne saw her now, he sure as hell would have had a heart attack, no matter his health condition.

Racing from behind the counter, Ava stormed off to catch up with Brianna and Paul. Just as her sister opened the door to DeWayne's office and held it open, so Paul would have to walk past her, Ava took Brianna by the arm, poked her head in the room right after Paul entered and said, "Please excuse us, Paul. We'll be right back." Calmly, she closed the door and, still holding onto Brianna's arm, Ava led her a few steps down the hallway away from the door. "What the hell are you doing?"

"What?" Brianna smiled. "I'm helpin' you out, sheesh." Her smile quickly changed.

A manner now reflecting a crudeness Ava knew as the real Brianna.

Her true nature was confirmed when her sister added, "Can't even say thank you, can you?" Rolling her eyes, Brianna yanked from Ava's grip, stuck out her barely covered hip and placed her hand on her waist.

"Keep your voice down, Brie. And don't give me 'what.' You know exactly what I'm talking about. Look at you!" Ava exclaimed.

"Ya know. You ain't the boss of me, Ava. Reality check—I run this place too." Looking down at herself, she added, "And just what is so wrong with me? I can't help it if you're jealous I can pull this off and you can't. I'm not gonna hide what God gave me."

Ava wanted to burst out laughing. Brianna was nothing but a joke. Instead, she took a deep breath and released her aggravation in a long puff of hot air. "Brianna, you can't represent the company dressed like this. You're *not* going back into the office dressed like a showgirl. Not to mention DeWayne would be furious if he caught you conducting an interview in what you're wearing."

"Whatever!" Brianna rolled her eyes again and started to walk off. Halfway to the exit, she came to a halt while wearing an odious look on her face. "You know, from now on, don't ask me to do you any favors." Shifting her body around, Brianna pranced off, leaving the same way she entered.

Ava shook her head and for a moment stood silently in the hall before finally heading back toward DeWayne's office to once again, take care of business…herself.

After taking a seat, Percival crossed one leg over the other and smiled. He glanced up at the ceiling and listened in on the conversation taking place outside the door.

If they only knew, he heard every word. He tilted his head to the side and frowned, noticing missing sheetrock and electrical wires dangling from the exposed rafters.

Not good.

Returning his gaze to the doorway, he tried to decide which of the two females he'd been assigned. Thinking of the two women, Percival acknowledged the challenges ahead. Despite whichever one needed his help, they couldn't have been more different. God assigned an angel to only one human. Ava for example, unmistakably the responsible one, even for one so young. She'd addressed him with respect and decorum while dressed in a professional light-blue sundress, which he must admit, did compliment her pulled-up brown hair.

However, the other one, Brianna? He laughed to himself. He knew her type instantly, the moment she walked in half naked. This female is one who would do anything to catch the attention of the opposite sex. Only as long as the man suited a certain appearance.

Percival purposely chose worn, ripped and stained clothing. From a far, Brianna shunned him. He heard what she said. Yet, he did seem handsome enough for her, once she got a better look at his features.

The first of many tests.

As predicted, one passed and one failed. From a distance, their human sight would only capture the appearance of his clothing, nothing more. So far, the evidence pointed in the direction of Brianna being his target. She certainly has some dark powers at work around her. Though, he didn't wish to exclude Ava just yet, he needed to give it more time. Sometimes, the appointed ones weren't the most obvious.

Percival noticed a picture frame on top of the desk next to him. He reached over and turned it around. Staring back, were Ava and Brianna flanking a tall man he would guess to be in his mid-forties. The man wore the brightest pair of yellow shorts he'd ever seen. He also held a sign out in front of him reading, in huge black letters, *'Kure Beach 2012 Spring Break Extravaganza.'* Putting the frame back in its place, he wondered if the man in the photo could be the owner he overheard Ava speaking about earlier. He felt sure the guy in the picture was not his assignment. Only the humans he initially contacted after his arrival would be the obvious choice. Finally rising from his seat, Percival took a few steps over to a small window. Sunset would come in about an hour's time.

What a miracle to see it again after so many years.

Angels were only gifted wondrous joys such as sunsets while on missions, which took them down to Earth. In the heavens, they never saw the beauty of sunsets. The Lord formed the sun in order to help man's planet sustain and prosper by supplying its warmth to the lands. Little did the humans know, the sun known as *Sheol* by God and his angels, had another purpose—to imprison tainted souls who were shunned at Heaven's gate.

Souls corrupted and poisoned by the works of the evil one, Satan, would then venture straight to Sheol upon their death. For centuries, human scientists proved the raging body of matter contained hot plasma and magnetic fields. On the contrary, those magnetic fields were to shield the depths of what the sun really contained and burned upon the fiery Hell of the sepulcher planet…a never ending nightmare of death and suffrage. Thus, the reason angels tried to save as many mortal souls as they could. Though, they could not save them all.

Percival stood in awe of the transforming sky of dark purple and pink. It pained him, knowing humans took it for granted. Too many souls went to Sheol in the past centuries. How he wished he could save them all. The angels were a creation of God. They'd never been human, or mortal. Spawned by God, they were without sin, but were capable of sinning. Their souls contained the purest form of life to aid in helping those who needed saving. Percival, who in his centuries of standing beside his Lord and Savior, watched angels try to aid as many humans as they could. With the human numbers rising, it became harder, but the angels would always be there, ready to save those who wanted redemption.

Percival pressed his fingertips on the cool glass, completely enraptured by the magnificence.

"The view is beautiful from here, isn't it?" Her voice sounded soft as a baby bird's song.

Turning around, his breath caught at the way Ava gazed at him. She looked lovely. Her skin seemed untainted by the damaging rays of Sheol. Yet, it possessed a soft radiant glow. Her brown locks of hair were pulled back into a ponytail by a blue ribbon accentuating the curves of her face. "Yes. It is quite a rare splendor to behold." He smiled.

"I'm sorry to ask you to come so late in the afternoon. Things are so busy for us during the day." Ava made her way into the room and stopped by his side, they both gazed out the window at the beginnings of the sunset.

Percival caught the light scent of her perfume, which reminded him of wild honeysuckle. Impure thoughts instantly entered his mind, and taken completely off guard by such deliberations, he tried pushing them away. However, his efforts were unsuccessful. Her beauty made him yearn to embrace her within his own power and strength, then caress her within his wings.

He cleared his throat, trying to focus on the sunset.

"I have never seen a more beautiful sunset than from this very spot. I guess that's why my uncle chose this room as his office. He could be found here at this time of day, every day. He liked to watch as the sun slowly fade behind the water. It's something he and my aunt used to enjoy together before she passed away. I never even got to know her." Ava turned, walked over to the desk, and picked up the photo he admired a few seconds before. "That's my uncle DeWayne, here, with me and Brianna."

Percival nodded. *Well, that confirmed the man in the photograph.*

Ava's expression reflected sadness as she continued to gaze at the picture.

Percival sensed her emotions and how sincere her feelings were toward her uncle. *This woman is certainly a rarity among humans, pure and untainted.*

"You see, my parents died five years ago. DeWayne is my mother's brother. Mine and Brianna's only living relative." Ava put the photo back in its place and turned to face Percival. "I don't know why I'm tellin' you all of this, it's just that there's something about you. I don't know. You seem like a person I could tell anything to." She shook her head. "Gosh that sounds crazy, doesn't it?"

"Not at all."

Ava blushed and seemed embarrassed.

He admired her honestly while inhaling the wild honeysuckle fragrance she emitted. Listening to her talk about her uncle's departed wife, Percival, without realizing, explored the slender frame of Ava's body. He cleared his throat again, trying his best to fight away the wishful desires. Angels never experience sentiments toward mortals. So why was he? She seems to be so truthful and trusting with a complete stranger. It's unheard of. Even he, an angel, felt enchanted by this woman.

Her lips are the color of ripened cherries. Oh, for the love of God, to taste such lavishing—No. No. What's come over me?

He gripped the wood of the windowsill firmly. Angels were not mortal, therefore couldn't share human emotions such as happiness and pain, Angel souls were pure and lived the ways of the Lord. Their time while on Earth only lasted until their assignment was complete. After doing so, they ventured back to Heaven, never to encounter the same human again…ever. If the angel failed to save the human's soul, they would lose their feathers and thus, the capability of their wings for all eternity.

A mark of failure.

"Paul, are you okay?"

Not realizing how long he'd stood silently, he swallowed hard. "Ava, I am deeply sorry to hear about the loss of your uncle's wife."

Ava glanced at the floor. "Thanks. If you'd like, how about we conduct the interview outside?" She quickly changed the subject back to business. "There's a cool breeze, and from the end of the catwalk you can catch a breathtaking view of the sunset. Although, I must warn you to be careful, some of the boards are loose. It's on my to-do list."

Percival watched as Ava tried to crack a smile. It wasn't very convincing, but he knew she tried to maintain a positive attitude. "That would be nice. And if I gain your approval for the job, you can hand that to-do list over to me."

A grin spread across Ava's lips at his gesture.

Percival swore he felt a jolt in his chest. In only a moment's time, how could one woman make an immortal, an angel, envy the living?

Chapter Five

$\mathcal{P}$ercival held the door open for Ava, then they both strolled alongside the length of soft white sand toward the catwalk. While they walked, he answered her questions about his qualifications. The years of experience, confirming his skills with plumbing, electrical and all types of construction work. Being an angel, he could do anything.

"You talk like you're from another world, almost," Ava noted. "English isn't your first language is it?"

Stunned for a moment, it didn't occur to him his pronunciation sounded any different, but being focused on an array of things, it must have slipped his mind he spoke so formal. "I—uh, I was not aware I spoke strangely. Does it make you uneasy?"

"See? That's what I'm talkin' about. Your tone is so proper. Like, well I don't know, but it's different. I see by your application you are a U.S. citizen. Have you traveled a lot and do you speak other languages?" Ava giggled. "I'm sorry. But if I'm going to hire you, it helps to know these things."

Percival grinned. "Yes, you can say I have traveled to different lands. And I speak many different languages. Do you?"

Ava laughed. "Heck, no. I've never even been to college. English is hard enough for me."

They both smiled and continued on their way.

"I guess I could tell you a little about the place. Let's see. We have two units we rent. East and west and sandwiched between, is the office building we just came from."

Percival nodded. "Yes. As I approached, I could tell the catwalk and the outside of the building are constructed of wood. And might I add, in dire need of repair."

Ava frowned and sighed. "Exactly. Which is why I must hire someone. Each unit contains five rental properties. Three one-bedroom suites on the first level and two larger, two-story suites, occupy the second and third levels. The two-story suites have floor-to-ceiling oceanfront panoramic views, including balconies. They are always the first to book."

Taking a quick glance behind him, Percival glimpsed both the east and west ends of the condos. While they continued walking toward the ocean, he had a better view. "Yes. I can see what you are talking about. Must be a great view from up there."

"I have to say, we do have a great location."

Finally reaching the end of the catwalk, they stood in silence for a moment, both staring out at the ocean.

The sound of the tide hitting against the shore sang in Percival's ears. Closing his eyes, he let his head fall back, took in a deep breath of salty sea air and listened to Heaven's miracle. Slowly opening his eyes, he turned and glanced at Ava who appeared to be in deep thought. Her attention focused intensely on the ocean, yet he would bet, she wasn't seeing its splendor. This strong young woman carried so much on her tiny shoulders. *Maybe I am here to aid her.* "Seashell for your thoughts?" He tried making her smile with his joke.

It didn't seem to work. Ava sighed. "The sun…have you ever wondered where it goes at night? I mean, I know it goes around the Earth, scientists tell us that. But do you think it's to show us darkness is the way of the world too? That not everything is bright, sunny and warm?"

Her words made him crave to take her in his arms and show her such warmth.

She continued, "Sometimes watching the sunset, I feel like all my hopes and dreams go down with it, sinking and drowning within the ocean."

Amazed at how deep this woman's soul ventured, he couldn't pull his gaze away. Then he understood the real miracle wasn't the beauty of the sunset, but the wonder of life itself he saw in the woman standing beside him—*Ava.*

"Wow. I'm sorry. Boy, this is pretty heavy for an interview, huh? I sure know

how to make someone want to work for us."
She frowned.

"On the contrary, it just shows how
much you need my help." Percival tried to
make her feel better. "I know this isn't part
of the interview and probably none of my
business, but just for the record, another one
of my skills is that I am a great listener."

At his remark, her lips lifted in a smile,
as she kept her attention focused on the
water. Then, her body visibly tensed and her
smile faded. "Oh Paul. I'll be honest with
you. This place is falling apart and it's my
fault. DeWayne is ill and I promised him I
would make sure the resort survived. This
business rests on mine and Brianna's
shoulders." A tear, too hard to miss, slid
down Ava's cheek and she raised her hand
wiping it away. "I can't keep this place up
and run it too. I just can't. My uncle worked
sun up to sun down, every day. Not a day
passed where something didn't require his
attention be it a clogged sink, busted water
heater, blown A/C to small appliance
repairs. And to top it off, if the poor man has
to hear one more complaint about a stuck
sliding door, I wouldn't have been surprised

to see him rip the things off their hinges and say, *'Welcome to the new open-view concept, y'all enjoy.'* DeWayne stayed on call twenty-four-seven before he got ill. There is just no way I can do all this alone." Ava shook her head and cupped her face with her hands.

Percival admired the way the ocean breeze loosened a few tresses of hair from her ponytail, which danced around her face. Normally, this would not be the best way of hiring someone, but then she wasn't talking to just *anyone*. Percival liked how she wore her heart on her sleeve. It showcased her vulnerability and honesty about who she truly was. He desperately wanted to say something, but the words at the tip of his tongue would make him sound crazy.

I'm here to help you. Your prayers will be answered. I am an angel from Heaven and will never leave your side until all is right.

Nope, that wouldn't go over well at all.

Ava slowly removed her hands from her face and turned to look at him. "We need someone like you. But it pains me I can't afford to pay you half of what you could be making somewhere else." Tears ran along her cheeks and she lowered her head.

Percival stepped closer and grasped her shoulders. Probably not a good idea, but he couldn't help himself. "I know we just met, but the person I see before me is strong, a survivor. There are greater powers in this world that *will* help you find your way. Trust in them. Have faith in them. As far as myself, I am at your service. You pay me what you can afford and that will be more than enough." Knowing he shouldn't have touched her at all, he placed a finger under her chin, lifting her head up, as their gazes locked. A spark ignited from such a small connection of flesh. A burning desire kindled deep inside him, a feeling like he'd never felt, till now. This woman needed him. The pull of her soul on his became overpowering.

Ava slowly began leaning forward, as did Percival. A strong force pulled them toward one another, almost as though fate itself wanted them to unite. Just as their lips were about to touch, Percival jerked back. "I—I'm sorry." He forked fingers through his hair and took a few steps back.

"No. It's me. Forgive me. Oh gosh, I'm a mess! How embarrassing. First day and I do this. Oh, Lord—look Paul, don't worry, I promise it won't happen again."

Her cheeks looked adorably flushed and Percival loved it.

She started to head back toward the office building. Then, after only a few steps through the sand, she stopped and spoke, "You start tomorrow, seven in the morning. We will discuss what your wages will be then. Goodnight, Paul, and…thank you." Then she continued on her way.

Percival stood there and watched until he no longer saw Ava's silhouette in the moonlight. Turning his gaze upward at the night's sky, he spoke to God, "If she is my assignment, to what purpose am I here to aid? I know it is not right to question, yet how is it possible I have reactions such as these?" Waiting…praying for an answer from above, he heard a voice coming from behind him.

"Well, hello there."

Percival turned around to find Brianna standing with her hands on her hips, still

dressed in the same attire, a sexy grin
plastered widely across her face.

Chapter Six

*A*t the end of the catwalk, out of

sight, Brianna watched Ava lean in toward the guy who'd come for the interview. Her body language suggested she wanted to be kissed. It amused her to think Ava would even think a hottie such as he would be interested in her. Brianna couldn't seem to remember the guy's name. A problem soon to be remedied.

Fluffing her hair, she watched until Ava made a complete fool of herself when the man suddenly pulled away from Ava's invitation.

Moron.

She waited until Ava was more than halfway up the beach and took matters in her own hands. *Time to seal the deal.* "Well, hello there," Brianna greeted as she stepped closer to him.

"Hello, Brianna." Paul said, although it seemed he kept looking in Ava's direction. Then he began to head down the catwalk away from the beach.

"Wait. Wanna talk for a while?"

"I'd like to, but I start work early tomorrow. I have to get some sleep."

"So, you took the job, how nice. Which means I'll get to see a lot of you."

The man stopped and turned around. This time, he looked Brianna dead in the face. "Yes. There is a lot that needs saving and redeemed around here." He smiled.

Something in his statement halted her in her tracks. Moments later, she realized she still stood there, alone. Brianna shivered as a cold chill ran up her spine, then she took off in the direction of her condo.

Percival bent over the catwalk with a hammer in one hand and a two-by-four in the other. With sweat dripping from every part of his body, he worked on replacing the damaged planks. He'd been at it since sunrise and even well past lunchtime, he still had twenty or more to replace. Weathermen predicted heavy rains by midweek and with it being hurricane season, he prayed the next couple of days he would finish and still be able to go over them with a UV protective stain.

Since the first night he arrived several days ago, he never received the answer he prayed for until after he listened in on Brianna talking about how they needed *him* because she'd been too busy.

Over the past few days, Brianna constantly complained about having to do dirty laundry, helping their maid clean rooms, and about how Ava always pestered her to help whenever guests needed things. "I'm not room service!" Brianna fussed.

Percival knew she never did them to begin with. He figured those were chores Ava assigned her to do around the place. Brianna's fit throwing always seemed to result in Ava doing them herself, which only angered him. It seemed to be Brianna's pattern. Ever since the death of her parents, this had been her innate nature.

Nails used for binding boards gripped firmly between his lips, Percival wiped perspiration from his brow with the back of his leather work glove. The summer had turned into one massive heat wave with temperatures soaring into the upper nineties. Come midday with no clouds found anywhere in the sky, the sweltering rays of Sheol caused Percival to strip from his white T-shirt and toss it to the sand behind him, just moments after he'd started working. The only article of clothing left were his jeans which clung to his lower body like a wetsuit.

While hammering away, he sensed approaching footsteps. He knew whom they belonged to. She always popped up out of nowhere. If he wasn't an angel and couldn't already sense Brianna coming, he sure couldn't miss her potent perfume. He didn't know what the name of the scent might be, nor did he care, but it smelled like she bathed in the stuff. Even out in the open, it choked him. It somehow made him think of Ava. Not in a bad way, but because Brianna was nothing like her sister—Ava reminded him of Heaven itself.

When he stood close to Ava, a light honeysuckle scent filled every pore of his body. Even after they parted, her alluring perfume lingered for hours and surprisingly made him desperately homesick. From the first day he arrived, when they stood together on the catwalk, watching the sunset, the way she looked at him felt as if her spirit penetrated him and took over. When he watched her walk away, she took him with her, having a hold on him like no other he'd ever encountered.

While Brianna's steps grew closer, Percival tensed. His soul curiously reacted in opposition to hers. It started the first night when she approached him on the beach. Her intensions were not sincere. Which meant one thing—this woman's soul must be influenced by the powers of Satan. Although, no one needed an angel to point it out. It followed her wherever she went. The moment her mouth opened and spoke, it became evident.

While witnessing the countless and heartless actions from Brianna over the past few days, it became clear she was the chosen one the Lord appointed him to help. The other day, he even overhead Brianna and Betsy, the maid, arguing about chores Brianna had been neglecting and Betsy called her on it.

"You told me you'd take care of the west units," Betsy stated.

"Well, I have other things on my mind right now," Brianna replied spitefully.

"You knew I was supposed to get off early today."

"Well…you'll have to take care of those rooms before you leave. I'm busy." Brianna turned to walk away.

"I *will* be mentioning this to Ava, Brianna. I know I only work here, but I'm not going to be treated with disrespect, especially by you."

Brianna turned around sharply, marched over and got into Betsy's face. "You say one thing to Ava and I'll fire you. Oh, and I'll make sure and spread the word about how untrustworthy you are, stealing from guest's rooms and from us. Just try me."

Betsy sighed, "May God have mercy on your soul. You are cold, Brianna." Then arguing no further, Betsy wheeled her cleaning cart through the walkway, heading over toward the west units.

Percival watched Brianna walk off in the direction of the beach with a wicked smirk across her face.

There were other times too, when guests had approached Brianna for assistance, only to be waived off as though they were a nuisance and she ended up leaving behind an agitated guest.

Now, it rested on him to guide Brianna toward choosing the righteous path.

Being assigned to her also meant Percival was Brianna's last hope and the only one on this planet who could save her soul. If he failed and she crossed over to darkness, there would be no hope, then Percival would sacrifice his most sacred attribute. He mustn't fail because the Lord's purity and sacred love for mankind depended on him. In his attempts to focus on helping Brianna, somehow Percival couldn't fight the urges drawing him to Ava. Her face crossed his mind constantly, ever since the night on the catwalk. Even now, he wished she would pass by, so he could catch a glimpse of her just once. But for the past few days, she was nowhere to be found.

"Well...well...workin' hard again today, I see."

The sound of Brianna's voice pulled Percival from his thoughts.

She walked by him and sat on the edge of the catwalk where he worked.

He paused to wonder if this woman had any other apparel other than bathing suits. Today, she flaunted her body by wearing a shiny platinum bikini with diamond rhinestones, outlining the tops of her breasts. Percival shook his head, thinking the difference between her and Ava seemed like night and day.

Brianna expected to be the center of attention. Out in the open, literally, where everyone would notice her. While Ava was the one you only saw in a flash of movement, if one were lucky, as she ran from one condo unit to the next, focusing on what needed to be done.

Percival hurt for Ava.

The work he did around the condominiums didn't compare to half the tasks she took on herself.

"Can I do anything to help, Paul?" Brianna giggled.

He knew she wasn't serious and he knew he needed to get used to being called Paul. He loved and cherished his spiritual name, Percival. A name appointed to him by his Lord and Master, but down on Earth, angels never used them. So, he chose Paul, a name close enough to his own. Unable to avoid Brianna, he took advantage of the moment and decided no time like the present to start saving her soul. Not glancing over to acknowledge her presence, he spit the nails from between his lips into his gloved hand. "You actually could help, if you truly wanted."

"Really?" She scooted closer. "What can I do?"

"It is not for me. It is for Ava. I am sure she is overwhelmed with things needing to be done."

Brianna grunted. "She's got everything covered. You don't need to worry about her."

"Well, I do and you should too." Percival bent forward, hammered a nail into the board, then stood upright. Wiping his brow, he asked, "My question is…why you are not helping?"

Brianna glared back at him, not showing one ounce of concern, as she simply sat on the edge of the catwalk playing in the sand with her French manicured toenails. "It's too hot, and besides, Ava has everything covered. She always does."

"You don't think it would mean a lot to her if you offered to help more?"

Brianna smirked, her hand covering the glare of the sun from her eyes as she stared at him. "Stop worrying about my sister. Anyway, I'd rather be here with you."

With a shake of his head, Percival realized their conversation was going nowhere. She didn't have any remorse about leaving Ava with the responsibility of managing everything. He certainly did have his work cut out for him. He turned his back to Brianna to drop nails into the toolbox. "Brianna. I—"

"Hey. You have a tattoo on your back. Or is that a birthmark? It looks funny. Most tattoos are outlined in black ink or something. Yours is a few shades lighter than your skin."

Percival paused. He couldn't give her the answer to his mark, but he wanted to continue their discussion about her sister. Even angels got agitated, but they never handled their missions with aggressiveness, no matter how difficult the case. So, he decided his next move would be the best option for both of them, for now. "Don't worry about the tattoo, it's nothing. I'm going to the office to get some water." Brianna opened her mouth to speak, but he added, "And to check on Ava."

His last statement seemed to trigger her anger, as she crossed her arms over her chest and got to her feet. Just as she turned, she mumbled, "Don't worry. You'll be mine soon enough."

Then she stormed off in the opposite direction.

Chapter Seven

A quick glance at her watch and Ava
shook her head. It's well past lunchtime.
Why did time fly by so fast? The day, as she
expected, would end the same way it
started—hectic. It began when her alarm
went off at four a.m. as usual, and after a
quick shower, a pick of clothing consisting
of a purple tank top and a white skirt with
flowers the same color as her shirt. Then she
headed directly to the office building to
open the kitchen. By five-fifteen, she set out
milk and orange juice cartons in ice, along
with different varieties of fruit in a room off
to the side of the main foyer…adding cream
cheese, bagels, boxed cereals and premade
muffins.

Although, they were a condominium and not a bed-and-breakfast, her uncle insisted they try and beat the competition by offering perks the other beach condo resorts didn't. So, DeWayne made one of the office areas on one side of the main building the breakfast/sitting area. The room measured at almost twenty-five by twenty-five and accommodated enough tables for occupants. Along one of the walls stretched a table made up of two coffee makers and stainless steel containers which held ice to keep the appropriate breakfast items cold. The decorated room displayed an array of beach accents and white wicker furnishings to make the place feel cozy.

While guests munched on breakfast before making their way to the beach, Ava took it upon herself to address some past-due bills requiring her immediate attention. She headed down the hall toward DeWayne's office. Unlocking the door, she flipped on the light switch, and sighed at the stack of bills sitting on his desk. "Gosh, I miss you, uncle." Taking a seat behind the desk, she started organizing the bills by their due dates, trying to address the ones more than thirty days past due, and stacking the others in an 'until more funds come in' pile.

Hours later, she glanced up at the clock to find it'd reached eleven a.m. Putting statements, receipts and accounting books in the top drawer of the desk, Ava got up to leave, locking the door on her way out. While walking, she glanced at the day's tasks, then dropped bills into the mailbox along the wall next to the front counter.

With Paul working on the catwalk, she didn't want to burden him with minor things she could easily address herself. In the Starfish Suite, a light bulb needed to be changed, one guest had problems connecting to the complementary Wi-Fi. Then two suites where guests had checked out yesterday afternoon, needed to be stripped of all bed linen and cleaned from top to bottom. Not to mention the regular daily cleaning to the rest of the rooms. Brianna's responsibility, along with their one maid, Betsy. As always though…Brianna couldn't be found at all. If she wasted time to search for Brianna, Ava wouldn't get her daily responsibilities accomplished, but if Ava needed to guess, she knew exactly where she would find Brianna. On the beach flirting with Lord knows whom. Finding anything to do that would take her away from helping Betsy and doing the day's chores.

By five-thirty in the evening, Ava finished all her duties for the day. Luckily, Betsy, being the saint she was, finished all the rooms too. Guests who stayed more than two nights, only needed their bed sheets changed every other day. So, the majority of the rooms only required the making of beds, vacuuming, mopping, disinfecting the bathrooms, as well as replacing toiletries like soap, toilet paper and tissue.

Entering the main building, Ava observed Betsy pushing a wheeled cart full of linens and heading to the laundry facility across from DeWayne's office. "Here, let me help you Betsy," she offered warmly.

"Thank you, miss." Betsy, at sixty-three years old had been with the condo resort since as long as Ava could remember...With a heart of gold. "What about Miss Brianna's room? I haven't cleaned it yet today. I was just about to go and—"

"No. I don't want you cleaning Brianna's room anymore. She's going to have to start doing it on her own. And no matter how much she begs, don't do her laundry. I'm sick and tired of her doing nothing around here."

At Ava's bitter words, Betsy replied, "Yes, ma'am."

"Oh, and Betsy, why don't you go on and head home. I can throw these in and get them started. It won't take long," Ava said, already starting to grab sheets from the bin.

"Bless you, Miss Ava. I am getting pretty tired. Plus, I'm not the young chicken I use to be." She chuckled.

"Well, then I insist. You've been on your feet all day. I can finish this and have these folded for you in the morning."

"Thank you, hon. I'll see you bright n' early in tha mornin'." Betsy went over to the lockers and unlocked one. Removing her purse, she shut and locked the locker, then left.

After loading sheets in one washer and comforters in the other two, Ava was done. Finally, with the washing machines going, she headed back to the kitchen to pre-bake tomorrow's breakfast muffins. At least one part of the business remained in good shape, thanks to DeWayne, when he actually installed a chef's kitchen. Although the appliances were secondhand and not state of the art, the kitchen seemed to be the only area not in need of repairs.

With the day just about over and while washing her hands, Ava gazed out through the window above the sink and caught Brianna's barley covered body over by the catwalk, undoubtedly flirting with Paul. A sudden pull at her gut made her turn away and head into in the pantry. She took out the all-purpose flour, oil, sugar, baking powder and a spice jar of cinnamon, then carried the items over to the middle island. Her stomach growled, but ignoring the hunger, she sat the items down carefully and went over to the refrigerator where she grabbed eggs, milk and a fresh box of blueberries.

After sorting them in front of her, she bent to open a cabinet and grabbed several muffin pans. The sound of the kitchen door swinging open, followed by heavy footsteps

made her peek over the top of the island.
She saw Paul's tall frame heading toward
her. She flushed as she always did in his
presence. With him working there for almost
two weeks, Ava thought the first night when
she almost kissed him would dissolve from
her memory. Yet, since that evening, not a
day passed when she didn't replay it over
and over in her head. Blaming it totally on
being mentally crazy at the time, but
somehow, she couldn't stop thinking about
him.

She'd offered Paul one of the condo
units, but he waved off her offer and said he
had a place to crash somewhere nearby.
Plus, he didn't want to take away from
possible income for the business. They did
agree on one thing, Ava would pay him in
cash. She knew the government would be
furious to discover this fact, but it wasn't
much. She still thought the amount wasn't
anything near what other companies could
afford to pay him, but Paul seemed happy
and she sure didn't argue the matter.
Daytime came and went like the wind while
Paul worked hard, taking advantage of each

second of daylight he could. She certainly appreciated all he did to help.

The time just after the sun set, became extremely lonely for her. During these down times, she appreciated more than just the maintenance work Paul did to bring new life to the condo resort. While she lay in bed, she would run her fingers over her lips wondering how Paul's would feel pressed against hers. Were they soft…hard? Would his touch be the same as his kisses? Ava shook the thoughts from her head more than once during those many nights since his arrival, allowing sleep to take her away from her daydreams. After all, why would he ever consider giving her one glance when Brianna strutted around the place like a neon sign?

"Aw, I see you are making blueberry muffins, my favorite...May I?" Percival smiled, making his way farther into the kitchen. He picked up some of the ingredients.

"Oh, I'm sure you have more important things to do than watch me burn muffins," Ava said, trying to smile. However, an image of him feeding muffins to Brianna

made her sick to her stomach. She noticed
Paul open his mouth to speak, but she raised
her hand, stopping him. "I know the catwalk
needs to be done before the rains come, so
don't feel you need to help me here. Also, if
you could try and *not* distract Brianna from
her duties, I'd appreciate it." Turning her
back to Paul, she walked back into the
pantry and returned with a mixer.

Paul was gone.

Her heart sank as she placed the mixer
on the island and sighed. Deep down, she
wanted him to stay, but worried about how
her company wouldn't compare to
Brianna's. Somehow, she didn't think she
could bear having him confess to her about
his feelings for Brianna, should he have
them. Not to her. Not when he ran across her
mind constantly.

Chapter Eight

 ℱinally, with muffins in the oven,
Ava finished washing and put away the
dishes. Placing the dishtowel beside the
sink, she turned on the facet and filled a
glass with water. About to take a sip, she
gazed out the window and found Brianna
sitting across from Paul again, at the
catwalk. Maybe he did prefer her company
after all. Which would explain his quick
departure after her earlier comment.

What really bothered her was where they
were. The edge of the catwalk where she
and Paul almost kissed. Yes, it was mainly
her doing and completely by accident.
Lonely, at not being around a man in so
long, she forgot herself that night, craving
what any lonesome woman would. Maybe it

happened because a man stood so close to her on a night when she needed someone. Like a warm security blanket…to have her fears vanish and replaced with warm, solid arms assuring her all would be okay.

Yeah, right. Fate didn't have a clue she existed.

She watched Brianna and Paul smile at one another, then something Brianna must have said made Paul laugh. Ava dropped the glass of water into the sink and palmed both sides of the basin. She lowered her head and tears slid down her cheeks. She knew she would never be his type. Not if he liked the kind of woman Brianna was. Seeing the man who gave her hope for one night, flirting with Brianna, tore at her insides.

Lifting her head, Ava couldn't help but continue staring at the two of them. Observing Paul wipe his forehead with his backhand, it didn't take a rocket scientist to pick up on how hard he'd been working. She shouldn't have been so rude before. She'd been nothing but short and bossy…no doubt another reason he preferred her sister. Since he'd started, she'd given him not one praise for all his kindness. There was no excuse for why she couldn't stop and say a simple thank you. It'd been because he made her nervous, so she tried to avoid him all this time.

Even from where she stood, she could tell Paul looked exhausted, and since there were no rain clouds to be found, hours had gone by with him toiling in the blistering heat. With her head up high, she took a deep breath, letting it out with as much valor as she could muster. She would do what any good person would do. She opened the refrigerator and grabbed a couple bottles of water. Taking the side staff door, she headed across the sandy beach toward the catwalk.

DeWayne built the catwalk many years ago, before she'd been born, to give guests easier access to the beach without having to tread through the hot sand. Plus, on occasion, they had guests stay who were in wheelchairs, so it gave them a way to access it with the other beachgoers. The wood planks were built a few inches above the sand. They started from the east and west units, connected in front of the main building and traveled the entire way to the beach.

Given the hot summer day and no breeze, Ava's tank top became glued to her back in a matter of minutes. Goosebumps formed across her body as beads of sweat ran from the nape of her neck and down her back. Bending over, she set the water bottles down. She then pulled up her long strands of hair, tying them into a ponytail. Retrieving the bottles, she continued toward Brianna and Paul.

The closer she got, the softer Brianna's words became, as if she didn't want Ava to overhear. Paul's appearance didn't change, however.

"Hi y'all. Today's one for the books, huh?" Ava said, trying her best to give off a friendly smile.

Brianna rolled her eyes and looked over at Paul, who stood and walked across the catwalk toward Ava.

"Glad to see you're in a better mood." He gave her a playful wink.

Ava noticed his beautiful set of pearl-white teeth shine in the sun like diamonds. "How's it coming?"

"As you can see…" Paul pointed at the catwalk. "…Progress is coming along. I should be done within the next couple of days."

"It really looks great, Paul. You are such a treasure to have around." Ava's body heated as the last sentence came out, and the sun sure as hell wasn't helping. Her heartbeat increased so much she heard it in her ears. "Oh, here." She held the bottle toward him. "I got you a bottle of water. I thought you'd need it out in this heat." When Paul reached out and took the water, their fingers brushed slightly. The same electric shock ran up her spine, just like the night when he lifted her chin. Paul's 'thank you', snapped her out of her lustful flashback.

Brianna glared at her "You didn't think to bring me one? That's really—"

"Yes. I did." Extending her other hand, she gave Brianna the second water bottle. Then, just as Brianna snatched it from her grip, Ava's vision blurred, followed by replacing both Brianna and Paul's image with black dots—then nothing.

It surprised Percival earlier to see Ava so uncivil. When she stormed off to the pantry, he sensed her jealousy and scanned around the room, stopping at the kitchen window. He put two and two together. She'd been watching him and Brianna, then assumed he had feelings for her sister. It bruised and astounded him at the same time. If he'd stayed in the kitchen, he knew he would've grabbed Ava up and into his arms in seconds. She seemed attracted to him, but remarkably, her cold treatment indicated she didn't care for his presence, and secondly, the one step he took toward her made him go rigid from an intense pain in his back. A deep sensitive twinge had him leaving the room quickly. He tried ignoring it, but the discomfort grew the more he thought about Ava. Percival didn't need to guess, it was a caveat as to the outcome should he stray off target.

His feathers were loosening.

Brianna was his mission, but even so, he felt drawn to Ava instead. A strange pull prompted him to want to help Ava, more so than whom he'd been sent to save. God is testing him. Trying to help Brianna ate at his gut, and he of all beings, shouldn't feel as he did. Why did he struggle so?

Why did images and thoughts of Ava consume him?

After leaving Ava so abruptly, he hoped when he returned to the catwalk, Brianna would be gone. Yet there she was, circling like a shark on its prey. He tried pushing Ava out of his mind by making small talk with Brianna. Evidently, she was his mission, so he tried probing at her soul. "So, tell me, Brianna. What do you do around here to help out?" Percival asked when he returned to the catwalk to work.

"Oh you know…things."

Of course, she would avoid the obvious question. "I hear your uncle is sick. Have you been to see him lately?"

She frowned. "Why would I do that? He's being taken care of by the doctors."

"Well, I am sure it would mean a lot to him if you went to see him? Show a little affection that you care? Have you ever thought about that?"

She paused as if she considered what he said.

For a moment, he thought he may have touched a nerve.

Wrong. Because she replied, "Ava's the saint in the family. I'll let her take care of that. She'll tell 'em hi for me. Why do we both need to say it?" Her attitude obviously flippant.

Her statement filled him with disappointment. To no surprise, he got nowhere.

Then a few moments later, Brianna's temperament darkened when she stood and glared at something over his shoulder.

Her expression amused him, because she never failed to show her inner nature, though she believed she hid it well from others. Only when he turned around and saw Ava approach did he look back at Brianna and he would swear the Devil stood before him. Hatred engulfed her soul with darkness and he felt it down to his angel core. It made him cringe at how this poor soul needed him more than he realized.

When Ava offered him the water, he realized her nature baffled him too, at times. Being an angel, Percival didn't really require water, but that didn't mean he didn't feel the heat from Sheol and perspire by its effects, which the water helped ease. Twisting the top to the bottle, his temper rose at the way Brianna sneered at Ava, assuming she hadn't brought her a bottle of water, when, in fact, she had. Those thoughts were replaced with concern when suddenly, he whipped around sensing Ava's temperature dropping. He rushed forward just as she fainted, catching her in both arms before she hit the catwalk. "Ava?"

"What a light weight. Can't stand the heat for one second," Brianna cracked. "Paul, she's fine, really. Just shake her, she'll come around."

"She fainted, Brianna. I'm taking her inside." Scooping Ava up into his arms, Percival took off at a fast walk.

Brianna muttered, "She's only doing that for attention, you fool."

He sadly expected nothing less from Brianna, but working on her soul would once again, have to wait. Pushing open the door with his back, Percival jogged down the hall toward DeWayne's office. He recalled a cot being there while he waited for his interview. Seeing the door cracked, he kicked it open and quickly headed over to the cot, gently laying Ava upon the makeshift bed. He brushed back a few strands of hair from her face as she began to come around.

Slowly, her gaze lifted and a set of chocolate-colored eyes, warm and comforting, stared back at him. Ava tried to sit up.

Percival palmed her shoulder, keeping her from doing so. "No. Lie still. You fainted. Give your body time to rest for a moment. Here…drink a few sips of this." Tilting the water bottle, he realized in spite of everything, it remained gripped in his palm, yet now almost empty from spilling the contents while carrying her. He placed it gently against her lips. "You need to find your strength," he said as his influence reached into her body. Percival looked for signs of why her body shut down. Lack of nourishment eased his mind at least her condition wasn't more severe. "I bet you have not eaten anything all day, have you?"

Ava shook her head.

"I see. Well, I will take care of this here and now. Do not move a muscle, young

lady, I will be right back." With those
words, he stood and darted out of the room.

Chapter Nine

She's gonna ruin everything! Brianna stormed into the building. Her anger rose as she scanned the hallway knowing Ava and *her* Paul were in DeWayne's office, alone.

She fainted on purpose to take him away from you! A voice said inside her head.

"I know!" Brianna exclaimed aloud.

Enraged, she threw open the doors to the kitchen. On the middle island, she spotted muffins cooling on wire racks. As if someone took over her body, she marched across the floor tiles and threw the muffins across the room.

"Little Ms. PERFECT! I'll show you!"

"What are you doing?"

A voice from behind her pulled Brianna from her fit of jealousy. "Paul. I was just…"

"You were just what? I have figured out your schemes, Brianna. You do not fool me. It kills me to know the person you are. What hurts most is your lack of concern for your sister. Has the devil corrupted you so much he took over your soul, too?"

"What!" Brianna's jealously rose to a level her body no longer controlled. "So you've chosen Ava, have you? I should have known Miss Goody-Goody would find a way to get her hooks in you. You're weak, Paul, you know that?"

"Weakness is only caused by those who surrender themselves unto darkness," Paul replied.

Brianna burst into laughter. "Ya know. You should've been a priest." Her sarcastic laughter continued. "By choosing my sister, you got nothing but Mother Teresa. You'll never know the wondrous pleasures I could give you. Are you sure you wanna give that up?" She trailed her finger from her neck to the middle of her bosom and with both hands ran her palms over her breasts and down her body until one hand stopped at her core. "Trust me. Ava could *never* please you like I can. You see? I'm the one for the taking. All you have to do is say yes."

Paul walked toward her.

He's finally gonna give in. She'd won him after all. Oh, how her holier-than-thou sister would react to see Paul had finally chosen the right sister. The *only* one who could satisfy a man's needs. Hell, Ava still walked a virgin for all Brianna knew, but she didn't care. There were no men who came around who didn't want her and if Paul didn't, he soon would if she had anything to do about it. This moment proved it.

Now, with only a few feet between them, he leaned in, and she closed her eyes, puckering her lips, eager for him to capture her mouth with his. Ready and willing to kiss him the fuck back. His lips never took hold. Brianna's eyes popped open. Paul leaned in all right, but only to grab a couple of muffins that luckily hadn't made it on the floor thanks to her earlier rampage. Brianna pushed him away with her palms with as much force as she could. "How *dare* you!"

Paul just stood there.

"No one turns *me* down, no one. Do you hear me?"

Paul laughed good and loud. He actually, released an outburst of laughter at *her*. "Brianna. Do you really have no feelings or compassion for anyone? I want to help you. I know there is a better person within you. Why won't you let those around you in?"

Brianna's temper rose and she stomped her foot. "And what makes you think I need help? Look around you, Paul. This place is falling apart and all you do is what Ava tells you. You can't honestly say you enjoy being her work-horse do you?"

Paul shook his head and sighed. "Man. Satan really has done a number on you, hasn't he? Is there nothing I can do to help guide you to a better place in your life?"

Brianna winked at him as her gaze scanned up along his body, smiling wildly.

"There is more to life than *that*." He groaned.

"How do you know until you've tried it?" Brianna wiggled her eyebrows.

"Sorry. Not interested."

Fury rushed from her feet to her temples with intensity. Brianna didn't like being rejected and nothing she tried seemed to get through to him.

"I feel sorry for you, I really do, Brianna. But for now, I need to get these to Ava," he said, holding up the muffins. "Goodbye." He started to exit the kitchen, then he turned. "I want you to remember something for me, will you? Myself and your sister will always have faith in you. We know the person you can be, Brianna. It is up to you to find your true self. Fight against darkness and turn toward the light of life."

Something struck her right at her gut. Did he speak the truth? His words stung, and for a moment, she wanted to believe. Is there a better version of her somewhere deep down? It didn't take long for that thought to fade the second Paul left the room. Brianna's egotistic disposition returned quickly, and poking her head out the door, she screamed down the hall, "I am myself, Paul. You need to get over yourself and step foot into the real world! I'll be here waitin'. You'll see. You'll come back to me!"

After what he said, she didn't believe the words she uttered would make a difference, but her pride was hurt. Fact of the matter was…the *truth* hurt. She couldn't let him know he'd gotten to her. So, doing the only thing that came to mind, Brianna ran out the side staff entrance and hunted for anyone who could give her what she needed.

Chapter Ten

*A*fter treading heavily up and down the shoreline, Brianna finally spotted her target. Changing her pace, she skipped forward, putting on her best smile and waved, as she got closer. "Hey, Marc."

What a wonderful coincidence to have found the guy who'd previously wanted to have *a little party,* just the two of them, when she ditched him for the hopes of catching Paul's eye. She'd seen him again a time or two and after asking a few locals around the beach, learned he and his brother were staying with a cousin for the summer.

When he spotted her approaching, the smile on his face felt like bait to a fish. She'd reeled him in all right. "Remember your offer a while back?" She ran her finger down along his chest. "Does it still stand?"

"Hell, yeah," Marc said excitedly.

"Well c'mon…follow me."

"Gotta run, fellas!" Marc yelled back to his friends, as he threw one of them a football he'd been holding.

Brianna took him by the arm as she led the way.

"So, where are we going?"

"My place." Brianna gave him a sensual smile.

Marc grabbed her ass. "Well then…lead the way, sexy."

It didn't take long for Brianna to get Marc behind closed doors. The second they entered her room, she slammed the door shut behind them and captured his mouth with hers. Wasting no time, she put her hand down his swim shorts and took his cock into her hand. He bit her lip on contact, then suddenly both began ripping the other's clothing off. Marc, with haste, untied the back of her bikini top and palmed both her breasts. Brianna moaned at his touch. Marc then bent and stripped her of her bottoms before removing his own.

"Take me. Take me now," she begged.

"You got it," he whispered back.

Both panting, he grabbed her ass, picked her up and slammed her back against the wall. He held her there with pure strength, his cock pushing against the inside of her hip. "I'm gonna fuck you till you scream my name."

Brianna took a fist full of his hair and jerked his head back. "Then what are you waiting for, fuck me and stop talking."

Marc grunted and slammed his cock deep inside of her, all the way to the hilt. They both screamed.

"Yesss," Brianna moaned.

He grunted alongside her cries for more.

Marc's rhythm increased with each thrust, faster and faster.

Brianna moved her pelvis along with his movements. "Oh yes…yes," she cried.

Marc then shifted without releasing her. Still sheathed within her, he moved away from the wall and headed toward her bedroom. Throwing her on her bedding, he smiled.

Brianna grew wetter as he pounced on her, flipped her over and took her from behind. He wasn't gentle and she loved it. She needed this. His shaft hammered into her and he pounded even harder than before. The sound of flesh against flesh echoed around the room, and at her moan of pleasure, she felt Marc's cock harden.

An outcry of release came from behind her as he shot his hot seed, filling her insides. "Woman, you're the shit!" Marc panted before flopping onto the bed. He pulled her next to him. "Give me a second and we'll go for round two."

Brianna laughed, squeezing his cock in her hand. "While we wait, why don't you tend to a lady's needs?" She leaned over and nibbled on his ear.

"My pleasure," Marc puffed while at the same time his hand found her core. He inserted several fingers, pulsing in and out while his thumb circled around her clit. His other hand took hold of one breast fondling it while his mouth found the other. With his tongue, he played with her nipple.

Brianna threw her head back and moaned while her body continued to be devoured by this man. Images of Paul entered her mind and Paul's face quickly replaced Marc's. His fingers, his hands, his mouth covered her skin. She felt the heat of her body rise and her lower region throbbed with want.

"Damn woman, you're wet…I'm so hard—"

"Not yet…you make me come before you get seconds, big boy."

Using his fingers, Marc almost drove Brianna off the edge. When she was close, he took her sweet spot into his mouth and the devil himself took over with his tongue. When she thought of it as Paul's tongue, Brianna came more than once. All the while, Paul's image not Marc's gave her the pleasures she'd been longing for.

While on her back, Marc straddled her and raised one leg over his shoulder. He inserted his shaft and went deeper and deeper. "Damn it you feel good." At those words, he slammed his cock further, thrusting in and out until the sounds of hot sex filled the room.

They had sex for hours, and finally, as they lay on Brianna's bed, Marc staring back at her, he asked a question she wasn't expecting. "What are you doing in a place like this?"

"Exactly." She grunted.

"You deserve much better."

"No shit."

"Word is your sister runs the place. Who chose her and not you to be the boss around there, anyway?"

Brianna grew angry and darted her gaze at Marc. "What makes you think *she* is the boss?" She jumped off the bed and snatched up her top and bottom. "I'm the boss around here too, ya know."

Marc jumped off the bed, "Look, I'm just sayin' what the talk is around the beach is all. Damn woman, don't get mad at me. I said you deserve more."

Brianna slowed her pace at getting dressed. "You do, huh?" She smirked. "And just how do you...?" Then an idea popped into her head.

Umm, yeah. Brilliant.

"Look. I have an idea. If it meant you and I could be rich and leave this place, would you be onboard?" Brianna said, strutting up next to him. She began rubbing his cock.

"I'd say if you keep doing that, woman, I'd be up for anything." He moaned.

"Good…meet me back here tomorrow afternoon, say five sharp?"

"I'll be here."

Brianna kissed Marc good and hard, securing he wouldn't forget.

Moments later, Marc left and Brianna stood in her living room with a sly smile on her face.

Yes…yes, this just might work. Finally, Ava will get what she deserves and Paul will realize who he should have been with from the start.

Chapter Eleven

Sitting on the cot, Ava took small breaths trying to regain her vision. As far as she could recall, she'd never fainted before. Thankfully, Paul caught her before she hit her head, or she would have probably ended up in the hospital as close to the catwalk as she was. With her and DeWayne both in the hospital and Brianna the only one—nope, she couldn't think about it. How careless she'd been not to have eaten all day. Her cheeks suddenly flushed as total embarrassment flooded over her. First, she'd been short with Paul in the kitchen, bringing him water to apologize, then fainted in front of him like a helpless child.

No wonder he probably prefers Brianna over me. I'm an ungrateful, can't stand the heat—weakling.

Annoyed with herself, she stomped one of her bare feet onto the floor and abruptly stood up from the cot. The sudden head rush made her unsteady as she grabbed hold of the wall, not to mention her head pounded like the entire percussion section of a symphony orchestra played in her brain.

A few moments later, the door squeaked open and Paul walked in holding two muffins in his hand. "Here. Eat these…and slowly." He held them out with concern written on his face.

"Thank you." Ava took the muffins and sat down again, taking a bite. "Hmmm."

"I know you are busy, Ava. But please promise me you will not go without food like this again. It is not healthy."

"I know, it was carless of me," she said with her mouth full.

"I am glad I remembered there was a cot in here." Paul smiled.

"Wait. How *did* you get in here?"

"The door was cracked, so I kicked it open, why?"

Puzzled, Ava stared at the door. "I know I locked the door after paying bills this morning. I *know* I did." She tried to get up from the cot.

Percival quickly rushed over and placed his shoulder under her arm, lifting her with his weight. "Easy now... Do not overdo it."

"I'm good. Thank you." Grateful for his assistance, she couldn't stop replaying the midmorning's routine, trying to rewind back to when she left DeWayne's office. Yes. She *did* lock the door. She remembered doing it. Right? The keys were still in her skirt pocket. Reaching into her pocket, she removed the set of keys and thumbed over them until she found the right one. Yes. It was with her the whole time.

"Wait!" Ava stormed across the room and ran over to the desk. Putting down the muffins, she picked up the photo of her, Brianna and DeWayne, then opened the back of the frame. There falling to the floor, another key to the office. Ava bent and retrieved it. She put it back into its place and set the frame down. Then she took out the accounting books and verified the last check number still remained in the business checkbook and pulled out the petty cash box. Nothing looked out of sorts. The last check number used was for their last grocery bill and the next available check number matched the accounting books. The receipt in petty cash was also correct.

Paul watched her closely a confused expression on his face.

Ava rubbed her temples, as her headache grew worse, if that were possible. The other third and final key to her uncle's office she placed in her room, inside her Bible. A location she'd thought Brianna would never look. Though now, she could be wrong. She frowned. "I just don't understand why the door wasn't locked." The throbbing pain took over and she felt nauseous. "I'm going to go lie down if you don't mind. I know there is still so much to do, but I—I just can't think. I have such a splitting headache." What she said was true, but she also wanted to check her Bible.

"Let me help you," he offered kindly.

"No. I'm okay. Really Paul, thank you."

The look on Paul's face told her he wasn't going to take no for an answer. After all, he'd helped her this whole time. If it weren't for him, she'd feel a lot worse if he hadn't brought her food. Rounding the desk to stand in the threshold of the door, she turned to find him watching her like a protective angel. She gave in. "Okay, fine."

Paul's face glowed with admiration as he advanced and held out his arm for her to take.

Ava allowed him to escort her to her room.

By the time they reached Ava's doorway, the pulsing sting at Percival's back felt so excruciating, he was certain he'd be the next to faint. The feather branded on his back, the one Brianna asked about earlier was not a tattoo. In fact, it was the mark of an angel of God.

Percival knew while he fought with the pain, he was failing his mission. The awareness of his feathers loosening and the feeling of doom grew much stronger now. He couldn't fail, he just couldn't. Though, some humans were too far gone, having been corrupted by Satan. They would not be healed. Angels tried saving all they could before they crossed that point of no return. At this moment, Satan did have more of a hold on Brianna's soul than he did. This distressed him deeply.

Escorting Ava inside, he glanced around and admired her choice of décor. Light blue painted walls, white trim around the glass windows. Nice hardwood floors with a white shag rug centered in the middle of her living room, complemented the soft white sofa and two mahogany end tables. Not one dirty dish found anywhere. It fit Ava perfectly, and Percival smiled. They headed down a hallway toward the back, where they entered her bedroom. The same colored walls, floor and her bed linen were all white. Her queen-sized canopy bed, made from the same wood as her living room furniture, was wrapped in white, see-through fabric. It reminded him of clouds in Heaven.

Ava released his arm and headed straight for her nightstand to pick up her Bible. She flipped through the pages until her fingers picked up a key. "I just don't understand," she whispered.

"What is wrong?"

"Nothing. I just need to lie down, I think." She returned the key and set the Bible back in its place.

Percival didn't accept that as an answer. He headed over to her. "Tell me. Maybe I can help." He took her by the shoulders and turned her around to face him. Their eyes locked. His heart began to pound faster and faster. The look in her eyes—something troubled her.

Neither one of them said a word, just stood staring back at one another. He watched her gaze trail to his lips, then back to his eyes. She did this more than once and so did he. They wanted the same thing. He pulled her in closer. She closed her eyes and he leaned forward. Just as their lips almost touched, the feather mark on his back fired up like his skin burst into flames. He pushed her away.

Her eyes popped open, the desirable gaze they displayed before now replaced with shame. "I think you should go." She turned from him.

He couldn't see her face, but he sensed her tears. "You don't under—"

"I understand perfectly, Paul. Just go."

"Ava—?"

"Paul. I said...go. *Please*."

Percival stood there for a moment.

Ava didn't move. She stood, facing her bedroom window, her back to him.

If he could only tell her how much he wanted her, yet he didn't have the words. The warnings of why angels were not to interfere with human fate. Finally, he turned and headed out of her bedroom. "I am sorry, Ava. I wish I could explain. But I—I cannot." With that, Percival saw his way out. Lingering for a moment outside her door, he rested his palm on the wood. His chest tightened at the sound of her locking it on the other side.

Chapter Twelve

$\mathscr{A}$ week went by, and Ava still felt puzzled at how the door to DeWayne's office had been open the day she fainted. A feeling something might be wrong alerted her senses. Over and over, she replayed what she'd done in her mind and knew she'd locked the door behind her after paying bills that day. To make matters worse, she couldn't stop thinking about Paul's rejection, either.

"That's it!" A cloud of dust drifted around her after Ava slammed her container of face powder down on the counter. She coughed. Sealing the top, she dropped her make up brush in a green cosmetic bag. Why should she even care how she looked?

Who was there to look good for? Still angry and hurt by Paul's lack of affection toward her, Ava couldn't focus on anything. She made sure she avoided him at all costs. She only checked in with him to check on the final progress with the catwalk and to start him on other things she needed done. Short and simple and with as few words and eye contact as possible.

Putting on a white sundress with small yellow flowers, she slipped her feet into a pair of white sandles, drew her hair up into a ponytail and finished it off with a yellow ribbon. Sighing at her reflection in a stand-up mirror, she snatched her purse from the dresser and headed out.

Walking along the sand toward the office building, she caught sight of Paul at one of the east end units, painting. She didn't give him a second thought, turning her attention back to the office as she entered to check and make sure everything was okay before she left. She took out the muffins and placed them in their regular morning spot for guests, followed by the usual boxed cereals and coolers filled with iced orange juice and milk, both white and chocolate. Her errand wouldn't take long and she would be back in time to put them all away.

With her keys in hand, she put a sign at the front office desk saying management would be back soon and below it listed a phone number for emergencies only. Ava exited the building. Brianna, of course, was nowhere in sight, so she got into her SUV and headed for the hospital to visit her uncle DeWayne.

The ride took only twenty minutes. Ava put on a strong face after speaking with the doctors and strolled into his room. "You look great, uncle. Doc says you might get to come home soon," she said, hugging her uncle around the neck and placing a kiss on his cheek. "You don't know how much we've missed you." *Well I have, anyway.* She kept the last sentence to herself.

Her uncle wasn't doing well. He now suffered with kidney failure. Tests reported his creatinine levels had reached nine, normal was between 0.6 and 1.3 milligrams per deciliter. And his BUN or Blood Urea Nitrogen, reached upwards of thirty with normal being seven to twenty-five. They needed to run more tests, and he would have to go through dialysis. When they told her, she started to panic, but the doctor's assured Ava her uncle would be okay. He would just be in the hospital longer than they predicted. The news wasn't what she wanted to hear, but as long as he would be fine, it eased her worries. The good thing was that he would recover. This would be the most imporant thing.

Surprised at her visit, her uncle tried pushing himself up in his bed.

Ava ran over to help him.

He smiled at her. "So. How's the business. Is everything okay? Do you need anything?"

Ava could swear the color in his face improved, as she shook her head and grinned. At least he sounded like himself. "Yes, everything is okay, Uncle. No, we don't need anything. In fact, we've had a lot of visitors lately. Business is good." She was sorta right. They did have visitors, but not as steady as she'd hoped for. They were still behind on a few bills, but she was determined to get them caught up before he got out of the hospital.

"How's Brianna? Why isn't she with you?" her uncle asked.

Ava didn't know what answer to give him.

Well let's see…she's either bathing in the sun, flirting with lord knows who…probably Paul…

Nope, she wasn't going there. "Oh, Brie is fine. She's holding down the fort so I can come see you. I hope you don't mind looking at my face." She smiled.

Her uncle held up a shaky hand and placed his palm on the side of her cheek. "My dear. You're always like a breath of fresh air." Then his smile turned into a frown. "I'm just sorry I took your youth from you. You should be running up and down the sand, chasing after boys and doing what pleases you."

They paused, then both started laughing.

"Okay, we both know that's your sister…but still. Ava, you're beautiful inside and out. I should have sent you off to college, so you could see the world. I sit here knowing what I've asked of you and it's not fair, I know. I promise I'll make it up to you somehow."

Tears swelled in Ava's eyes. "No—no, Uncle. Stop." She wiped away her sorrows and leaned down hugging him. "Please. I'm good and I'm happy. I wouldn't have things any other way." She pulled back and using a napkin, dabbed her uncle's cheeks as he too wept. "Okay. I didn't come here to make us both cry." She sniffed, straightening herself up. Picking up a beige plastic cup, she poured water into it from a Styrofoam pitcher. "I'll be right back, Uncle. I'm going to go ask the nurse for more ice chips."

She needed a moment to get herself together. Hospitals never were her favorite place. It was where she was told her parents were taken and pronounced dead after their car accident. Her uncle had come and identified both bodies. Ever since, hospitals weren't her favorite place to be. She wouldn't be able to handle it if her uncle passed too…But Ava couldn't even think about it. She went to get him a pitcher of ice chips.

Back in the room, she placed the pitcher on his meal tray and sat beside him on the bed. "Now. Tell me. What have you been doing to keep busy? Not flirting with the nurses, I hope. Even though…" Ava looked over her shoulder. "I think nurse Janet has a thing for you." She giggled.

"Ava…please." Her uncle blushed. Then he looked up at her and smiled. "You really think so?"

She burst out laughing. "Uncle, you're too much."

"She is a looker." He tried laughing, but started to cough.

"Now…now…don't get excited. I know you like the nurse, but this isn't how I want you getting her attention." Ava got up and pulled the sheets tighter around him, then tucked them in on the sides. "I'm going to go. You need to rest. I'll give you a call and check on you later, then I'll come back to see you again in a few days." She leaned in and kissed him on the forehead. "I love you very much. Take care of yourself, and when you get out of here, I'm going to throw you a big party. And I might just invite nurse Janet…if you're lucky." She raised her eyebrows, snickering.

Her uncle smiled and kissed her on the cheek. "You make sure and take care of yourself, too. You look tired. I wish I was well enough to—"

"Now, I told you to stop worrying. I'm fine. I even hired a guy to help out around the place doing maintenace stuff. So, don't you worry about a thing. Just get well." She didn't go further into the details about the guy. Honestly, she didn't want to say his name, only to ease her uncle's mind she wasn't the one handling such things around the place.

On the drive back, Ava thought of her uncle lying in the hospital bed. She prayed the doctors would find a way to get him well—and fast. She didn't care if he ever worked again, she just wanted him home.

Chapter Thirteen

"I'm throwin' a beach party!"

Brianna blurted at Ava the moment she walked in the front office door from her visit at the hospital.

"You're what?" Ava asked, annoyed. Still distressed by the visit with her uncle, she certainly wasn't in the mood for this.

"I'm havin' a party. Tomorrow night. I'm invitin' everyone along the strip."

Ava shook her head in disbelief and stopped in the middle of the foyer. "Brianna, we don't have the budget for this."

"Oh, c'mon, sis. We can come up with a few hundred to throw a small party. Everyone will bring their own beverages and we can supply music with our outside sound system. What more do we need to provide?

I'll even have Paul chop some wood for us, so we can have a huge fire pit on the beach. It'll be fun."

Ava couldn't believe what she was hearing. Tired and drained, as her visits with her uncle usually went, she couldn't deal with this too. "Brianna. What about the food, condiments, plates, cups and so on, associated with throwing a party? Have you thought about that?"

"Oh, we can pay for it and write it off as a business expense."

"You know what? I can't deal with this now. You do what you want. But hear me when I say this…you're not using one penny from our business bank account. If you want to spend money on a party, you'll have to pay for it from your own pocket and the company will *not* reimburse you. I think there's about fifty dollars in petty cash you can have, but that's it. I'm sorry. We just don't have the money. If you paid any attention at all to how things were going around here, you'd know this."

"FINE! Whatever. Oh, and I'll need a key to uncle's office, so I can get the cash.

That's if you don't mind?" Brianna rolled her eyes.

"Here, go and get it, but lock DeWayne's door after you leave and bring me back my keys. And I want them back today."

Brianna snatched the keys from Ava's hand and went in the direction of DeWayne's office.

Going with business, Ava headed over to the breakfast area and started cleaning up the early morning spread. All the muffins were gone, as usual and thankfully, there was still ice left covering the orange juice and milk. After she put all the things away, she mustered up enough strength to start on the next day's muffins. Before she'd call it a day, she would stop by DeWayne's office and pay a few bills, go through the incoming mail, as well as check any voice mails. It suddenly came to mind she needed to make a few calls of her own to confirm a few reservations made a couple weeks ago. After all that, she'd finally head to her room.

Step by step, threading his way through the white sand, Percival headed toward the party. A huge bonfire crackled, devil's flames reaching high into the night. With only a day's notice, Brianna had added to his list of duties. She needed wood chopped. When he questioned her why on earth she would need so much wood, she mentioned she was throwing a party the next night. Then before she left, she made sure he knew he was invited, too.

His only reason for showing was to check and make sure everything went okay. Plus, to make sure the embers didn't catch anything on fire. He didn't trust Brianna one bit to look after such an important detail. Shaking his head, he wasn't surprised to find zero pails of water placed in safe spots just in case. One would think with an ocean nearby, they wouldn't need water, yet once flames started spreading, the ocean wouldn't help. After filling a few iron cans of water, he placed them near the pit. Everything else seemed to look okay.

It didn't take him long to spot her. Brianna stood out like a sore thumb as she danced around the blaze, like a demon in heat, gathering the attention of all the males. Obviously, what she intended from the start. Although, his focus should have been on Brianna, he couldn't help but catch Ava, sitting on a log, far off from the crowd. Staring down into a cup she held with both hands, he approached slowly, yet something made him stop. Percival gasped at how striking she looked.

Her shoulder-length hair looked like silk cascading down her shoulders and back. It felt as if this was the first time he'd ever seen her. He couldn't recall ever seeing her with her hair down. A few strands blew in the night's gentle breeze. If he stood gazing at her for a century, it wouldn't be long enough to admire her beauty. In that moment, Percival realized his feelings. Afraid to accept them, yet he couldn't fight the hold she held on his soul. A temptation came over him to embrace how he'd come alive since his arrival, and it was all because of her. He stood unable to proceed, knowing full well the reason for his hesitation.

That night several days ago remained fresh on his mind. They'd almost kissed.

Contact would have been made, if not for the warning. The mark of the single feather below his left shoulder blade signified what it would cost him; therefore he broke away from the luring temptation. The damn thing stung even now, just thinking of what her lips would have tasted like.

I know…I know… Percival gazed upward at the star-infested sky. *They* never stopped watching.

With a deep sigh, he turned around and headed in the opposite direction. A good walk down the beach wouldn't cure his ailments, but space between them might be the best he could do for them both. When his feet reached the edge of water, a giggle had him turning around.

Brianna stood, well if you could call wobbling and swaying back and forth…standing. Drunk and beside herself, she jumped and threw her arms around Percival's neck, covering his mouth with hers.

With both hands, Percival reached and took Brianna by her shoulders, pushing her back. "What are you doing?"

"Takin' what I want. You know you want me, Paul. Just admit it." She slurred her words, which were followed by a hiccup.

"Brianna, you are drunk."

"So."

"So! You need to go home and sober up."

"I'd rather be here with you."

Percival sighed. "Brianna, I am not interested in you. Do you not see that by now?"

Brianna stomped her foot and hiccupped at the same time. "I know you want me, Paul. I can tell when a man likes me. You want to play hard to get? Fine, I can play that game." She tripped, caught herself with both hands in the sand, then quickly stood upright.

"Brianna. Go home." Percival pointed toward the condos.

"Help me?"

"Help you what?"

"Help me home." Brianna smiled.

Percival wasn't falling for her act…just a lure to get him into bed. "You will be fine." Her condo was in plain sight from where they stood. He turned to walk off.

"Don't walk away from me, Paul!" she screamed from behind him.

While he continued putting distance between them, the last thing he heard from her was, "You'll regret this. I promise you!"

Chapter Fourteen

After walking for blocks toward city life, Percival stood in front of two double doors and took a deep breath. Taking their long bronze handles in both hands, he swung them open and entered. A spiritual setting welcomed him as he headed down the long red, carpeted aisle. Passing dark mahogany pews, his gaze lifted and admired the array of beautiful stained glass windows. Stopping at the altar, he bent on one knee. Looking to the left, right, then behind him more than once, he searched out and sensed he was alone. Revealing his wings, he flapped them behind him. His head lowered when he noticed he'd lost more feathers. So far, it was evident…he wasn't succeeding in his mission.

Percival raised his head and stared up at a large wooden cross, hanging on a wall above where the choir sang their hymns. He prayed. "Lord, I need you. I struggle so, in my hopes of helping the one who You sent me here to aid. She is not the failure, I am. I cannot seem to reach her. I know I am failing in more ways than one. The other human sister…Lord—I cannot get her out of my mind. She is occupying my every thought and challenging emotions I never knew I had nor felt until this day. I fight against temptation and it is killing me at how fierce her hold is over me. Why do I struggle with this? Am I not an immortal angel, one who does not contain such affections? If I am being challenged, please help and guide me along, so I do not fail You. For my mission is clear, in my soul, I do not wish to go astray from the task. Help me, oh Lord. I am Yours to command."

For a long time, he stayed kneeled in the same position. He didn't expect God to respond. After being tempted by Satan's indulgences for so long, Percival just needed to visit the closest place to home. It always felt good to stand in the house of God.

In deep thought, he continued to pray silently, when suddenly a presence drawing near made him whip around. Quickly, he concealed his wings. No doubt it wouldn't go over well with the man upstairs to have him caught standing at the altar for all to see. Humans believed angels existed, but they weren't ready to see one this close. Still, to his surprise, there standing at the end of the aisle—

Ava.

After eyeballing her cup of beer, not having taken one sip, Ava poured the liquid in the sand, tossing the cup into a garbage can. Then she went to take a stroll along the beach. Enough light from condos, restaurants and cafes accentuated a soft glow along the shoreline. Plus, with the full moon, it made it a perfect night. Too bad, her mood didn't reflect the same. While walking along the spongy sand, she wrapped her arms around herself feeling thankful she'd chosen a thin, white sweater. The cool evening breeze added the perfect ending to a hot day, but if she stayed out too long, she knew it would turn chilly.

Heavy thoughts invaded her mind—her uncle's health, the business, mixed with her recent feelings toward Paul. Laughter and screams of intoxicated men chasing half-naked girls around the beach echoed behind her when strangely she heard two familiar voices up ahead. They were a little ways in front of her, but thanks to the moon, it seemed it wanted to highlight the scene taking place. A couple stood lip-locked and just whom the two were was all too clear. Ava took off running, upward from the beach and in the direction of urban life.

She finally came to a stop. With her palm resting against a brick building, she tried catching her breath and shaking the image of Paul and Brianna kissing. How stupid she'd been. It was obvious he'd chosen her sister. At least she no longer needed to hold onto the hopes Paul could possibly have feelings for her.

Sadly, with her head hanging low, Ava walked through the small town watching loud crowds of party-goers running up and down the streets, laughing and having a good time. She couldn't go back, not just yet. She stopped at one of the open cafes and listened to a one-man band sing, and play saxophone. She recognized a few songs and with her love of jazz, she stayed and listened. When the musician started to sing, *I've Got A Woman* by Ray Charles, she felt tempted to leave. Tears flooded her eyes. The man's voice moved her and she could have sworn if she closed her eyes it would be Ray Charles himself. The words and their meanings soaked in—damn, how she wanted Paul there with her.

Next, he started singing *Nothing Can Change This Love* by Sam Cook, and Ava did finally leave. She couldn't take anymore. Her heart ached and if she stayed any longer, she would find herself at the bar doing more damage than not. So, the best thing she could do was head in the direction of the only place that gave her comfort when she needed it most.

Opening the double doors, she did a double take.

Why lord. Why are you doing this to me?

The look on his face—he seemed just as surprised to see her.

Looking around the church, she didn't see Brianna. "What are you doing here?" Ava said, walking up the aisle.

Paul turned his head, looking away from her.

She stopped in her tracks. "Paul?"

"Why does God test me as he does?" he said, pounding his fist against the wooden podium.

"What do you mean?" Ava asked, taking small steps forward.

"STOP!"

Ava froze in her place at the tone of Paul's voice echoing in the house of the Lord.

"I am sorry—just. Don't come closer. I…"

"Is something wrong, Paul?"

Paul turned his gaze while never looking up. It remained glued to the ground and he stormed off in a mad rush, marching down the aisle, never stopping once he reached her.

Ava touched his arm, but he didn't halt his angry stride. "Paul! Paul!"

He never looked back.

Seconds later, Ava stood inside the church alone. Her gaze moved toward a wooden cross hanging above a choir section. She made her way down the aisle, then stopped and got on her knees. Looking up at the cross, she started to pray. "Lord. I don't know the purpose of the tests You put in front of us. I guess it's to make us stronger so we can deal with obstacles in our life, or to be strong for more than just ourselves. Help me to continue to be strong for my uncle. I pray, You give him as little pain and suffering as you see fit. I would like him well and home with me, Lord, but if You should need him, please give me a little more time with him. That sounds selfish, I know. Forgive me, but you see…"

The church remained quiet all around her as though time had stood still.

Ava fought back tears. "He's all I have left. If You take him away, I feel I will fall apart. Lord, I pray for my sister. She has never accepted the loss of our parents. I truly believe it's why she does what she does. It blocks out all reality for her, because if she has to face it, everything would be real, even accepting our parents are not alive, and she doesn't have the strength. Please help her, Lord. I love her so. And Lord, thank you for sending us Paul. You answered my prayers the day you sent him to me. Whatever ails him, I pray he receives the answers and guidance he seeks from You."

Chapter Fifteen

Three antagonizing days went by and Percival could take it no longer. As an angel of God, he had no reason to treat Ava so coldly, especially in the house of God. The moment he sensed her, something snapped. Is he being tested? Did Satan send her to test his abilities, so he would stray from his task? Is God watching to see if he passed or failed? Tests…tests…everything is a test. The more time Percival spent on Earth, the more he felt as though he might be going mad. Torn between two sisters, one whom his mission is to save her soul, the other enticing him with hidden desires.

Percival threw the paintbrush he held in his hand and kicked the can of dark stain.

The liquid splattered everywhere, snaking its way through the sand.

"Well…It seems we're still angry about something. But please don't take it out on the paint supplies."

He didn't realize Ava had been watching. "I am sorry. I will clean this up and—"

"Paul. Have I done something?"

He couldn't face her. "No."

"Then why don't you tell me what's wrong? You're different now. If it's about your feelings for Brianna, you don't need to worry. It's fine. As long as you both are happy, I—"

Percival whisked around so fast, he almost lost his balance. "What? You think your sister and I—it is not like that at all. I am *not* with your sister, nor will I ever be."

Ava put her hand to her forehead and shook her head. "I don't understand you, Paul. You almost kissed me. Then you push me away. Next, I see you kissing Brianna, and *now* you say you're not into her?" She turned away from him, took a few steps, then turned back around. Her expression wasn't friendly. "Stop playing games. Can't you see I have feelings for you?" Moisture swelled in her eyes. Ava ran from Percival, tears flowing freely down her cheeks.

The scent of tears triggered a sharp pain, piercing through Percival's chest. He stormed after her. Little did she know, he was sacrificing everything. He no longer cared if he was being tested. She only got a few feet down the beach before he grabbed her upper arm gently and spun her around. He wallowed in agony from the power Ava held over him. "I do not want Brianna. But I cannot…"

"I know—I know. I don't want to hear excuses. I've heard them too many times."

"You do not understand." Percival didn't know how to explain. Fighting emotions was new to him. Still, he couldn't lose her.

Ava broke from his hold and slowly walked toward the ocean.

Percival didn't fight back, but he did take a step forward in hopes of going after her. Then, the sharp pain in his back contradicted his actions. Suddenly, he heard a voice not of Earth.

Do not go after her, my son.

Brianna peeked inside the hospital room. Marc followed close behind her, dressed in a tailored suit. The room was silent. The only sound came from machines hooked to her uncle as he slept in the hospital bed.

When she approached, he slowly opened his eyes and smiled at her. "Brianna. It—it's so good to see you." He coughed. "This is a—pleasure. Ava didn't tell me you were stopping by—today."

Confused, Brianna asked. "Ava's been here?"

"Yes. She comes here every week. Y—you didn't know?"

"Yeah, sure…But my visit, I'm afraid, is of a discomforting matter."

"What do you mean?" DeWayne's smile changed to a perplexed expression.

Brianna sighed and made her way to the side of his bed. Her high heels clicked on the tile floor while Marc stood silent in the doorway. Brianna stared at her uncle with sad eyes. "Well, I didn't want to worry you with this. But due to the situation we're in, I felt the need to come by and see you."

"What's—wrong?" DeWayne tried pushing himself up against his pillow, but seemed to be too weak.

"Here, let me help you." Brianna helped him sit up straighter in the bed and leaned in, placing a kiss on his cheek. "Well..." She signaled for Marc to come closer, "I didn't want to have to do this, but the resort is in trouble. Ava's been stealing money."

DeWayne began turning paler. "No. I don't believe it. She wouldn't."

"Yes, she would, and did. I'm sorry, Uncle. But it's why I needed to see you today. I brought A.J. here with me to help. If you sign these papers, you can give me control and I can have Ava arrested. It's the only way to save what little she hasn't stolen and destroyed already."

"No. The bank would have come to me." DeWayne shook his head in disbelief.

"That's just it. Ava told the bank she needed cash for a party she threw a few days ago. She needed funds in petty cash. So, she's been withdrawing from the business account."

"No...no. She would never—"

"Uncle, you've got to trust me. I came here to help you stop her. I can't let Ava do this to you. Look at what you have done for us." Brianna began pacing around the small room at the end of his bed. Every few seconds, she would glance at him from the corner of her eye.

DeWayne never moved a muscle. Finally, he sunk into the mattress and a tear trailed down the side of his face. "I don't believe it. I just...don't believe it."

Brianna hurriedly went to the side of his bed and placed a hand on his arm. "I know, she had us all fooled. The best thing now is to sign these papers, so you can put a stop to this." Anxiously, she watched him. With shaking hands, she pulled a meal tray toward his chest and slid the papers closer to him, clicking the end of a pen.

Timidly, her uncle leaned over, holding the pen in his frail fingers, the point of it on the signature line, he then lifted his head and stared at the wall in front of him. He dropped the pen. "No. I won't sign these. I want you to call Ava. Then, I will call my lawyers. I want them all here, now."

Brianna stood, agitated.

Then Marc spoke, "I'm sorry to say you don't have an hour to spare, Mr. McKnight. If you read the document, you'll see your attorneys are already aware of this detail. I'm from their office. The doctors wouldn't allow everyone to come due to your condition. Brianna spoke with them and they sent me on their behalf. Their council was beseeched and this is the last resort.

"I don't care what you say, boy. I want to hear it from my lawyers, myself. I also want to speak to Ava," DeWayne argued.

Brianna bit her lip. They didn't have any time to spare.

Chapter Sixteen

"*We* predict Tropical Storm Ben

will become a Category 5 hurricane with wind speeds reaching over one hundred and fifty miles per hour. It will hit the shores of North and South Carolina, along the Wilmington and Myrtle Beach areas. Looking at the time charts we have here, if the intensity of this storm stays strong, we are looking at it becoming a Category 5 by tomorrow evening. We advise everyone in these areas to seek shelter and…"

Ava muted the television. "Did you hear that?" She looked over at Brianna. "We need to start putting things away and board up the place, now. I will alert the remaining guests who wanted to wait it out. They'll need to pack up and leave by tonight. We can't risk their safety."

Looking around, she could see a lot needed to be done and Ava didn't know how she'd do it all by tomorrow. Two days ago, she'd heard a storm was coming, but the last report had it listed as a tropical storm, just strong winds and rain. They were used to those. "Brianna. I need you to make sure all the umbrellas and lounge chairs are put in the storage unit, I don't think I got them all the other day. We also need to strip the linens and unplug all the electronics. Oh, and board up all the windows. Gosh, I didn't think it would get this bad or I would've done all this days ago." Ava turned off the television and sighed. "Plus, I guess we'll have to stay in town until this passes. I'll go find Paul. We'll need his help to get this done faster."

Things with her and Paul hadn't changed. She told him how she felt on the beach. That's where the conversation ended. Since then, it'd been business as usual.

"I'll go find Paul. You go and take care of the guests," Brianna said, running out the staff side entrance.

Ava didn't have time to worry about the real reason Brianna offered to go find Paul. Right now, she had other important things on her mind. She headed to the other side of the building, toward the east end units and started knocking on doors. The winds already kicked up a notch. She could barely keep her balance. With her clipboard in hand, she had the list of the guest's names and the number in their party who hadn't already left. One by one, she addressed them all, glad to see they were already packed and planning on heading out within the hour.

Turning a corner, she gripped the outside wall for stability. The winds were picking up. Ava headed toward the west end units when she smacked into Paul. "Oh. Paul."

"In a hurry, are we?" He smiled.

"Have you spoken with Brianna?"

"No. Why?"

"I'm sure by now…" She peered up at the sky, "…I don't have to tell you a hurricane is coming. I'm going to need your help with some things, but most importantly, with boarding the windows up. Can you help?"

"Of course. Just tell me what you need me to do."

They both stood there silently, gazing at one another.

"Umm. Well. I'm sure Brianna hasn't done it, so can you go pull the remaining umbrellas and lounge chairs and stack them inside the concrete storage room? Then lock it up." She reached into her jeans pocket and pulled out a set of keys. She removed one from the ring and handed it to him.

"Sure. I will go right now."

Ava stepped forward to leave when he took her by the arm. "Ava?"

"Yeah." She gazed up at him.

"There is something I want to tell you."

"Okay."

"There you are," Brianna said, interrupting. "I need help with the umbrellas. They're too heavy and these winds are messing up my hair," she whined.

Ava shook her head and grinned at Paul.

Paul rolled his eyes. "Coming…" Then, he leaned in and whispered, "We are not done."

"Another time, then?" Ava asked as Brianna yanked Paul away.

With the guests in the west units warned and supposed to be gone within the hour, Ava passed Brianna's unit and noticed her door stood wide open. A strange feeling grew in her gut and she looked left and right along the stairwell. It'd been close to an hour since she'd left Brianna and Paul. Slowly, she walked closer and peeked inside. "Brianna?" she called out.

Maybe Brianna hadn't closed it well enough and the winds had blown it open. The living room light was on, so she entered. On alert, she scanned the room. Everything appeared to be in its place. Thankfully, the winds hadn't caused damage. All appeared as it should be. About to leave, she jumped when papers suddenly came loose from under a glass sitting on the coffee table. She rushed across the room to retrieve them. She did a double take when she caught sight of a purple sticky note that read, *"We can't wait any longer. I forged your Uncle's signature and it looks freaking identical. Am I good, or what? Call me—Marc.* "

Scanning over the pages, Ava thought she would pass out right then and there. She swallowed hard, not believing what she was reading. Fisting the sheets of paper furiously in her hand, she stormed out of Brianna's room, slamming the door behind her.

En route for the office building, there was one thing she needed to do first. She ran down the hall toward DeWayne's office where her purse sat locked in one of the drawers. She unlocked the door and ran behind the desk. Inserting a key into the drawer, she opened it and dug inside her purse then pulled out her cell phone. About to go to her contacts, when she noticed a missed call from her uncle.

Good. She needed to have a conversation with him. She hit the call-back button, and the phone dialed DeWayne's hospital room.

"Hello?"

"Uncle. Something's happened and I don't know what to do!" Ava said, hysterical.

"Calm down. I hoped you'd call me back. Is it about Brianna's visit?" he asked.

"What? She came to see you?"

"You know, she said the same thing when I told her you came to see me. Don't you girls talk?"

"Uncle, there's so much I haven't told you, because I didn't want to worry you. Brianna isn't who we think she is."

DeWayne sighed. "That's what she said about you."

"What?" Ava sank into the office chair. "Oh, Uncle!"

"Tell me, what's wrong?" he asked

"I found some documents in Brianna's room. I walked by her door and found it open. I figured it was due to the heavy winds blowing through, so I went to check it out and that's when I saw some papers. I skimmed over them and they look like legal documents where you're handing the business over to Brianna."

"What?" Her uncle's raspy voice came over the receiver.

"Wait. There's more. Another document states where Brianna is selling the place for two hundred thousand and all the documents have your signature on them."

"I don't believe this." DeWayne sighed over the phone.

"I know. There's a sticky note on the first page from a guy named Marc. He's the one who forged your signature. Do you know him?" Ava asked.

"No. Brianna stopped by yesterday. She had a man with her from my attorney's office, but said his name was A.J. I had never met the guy before. I called my attorney's office this morning and they've never heard of the man either. Ava, Brianna accused you of squandering money from the business."

Ava couldn't seem to speak—her own sister. A part of her wasn't surprised. Brianna had never been the same since their parent's death. But how could Brianna have done this to DeWayne? After all he'd done for her. During those years, he'd always been there for her. He'd picked her up at the police station for shoplifting once. Not to mention the number of times DeWayne had driven up and down the city streets at all hours of the morning trying to find Brianna after she'd missed curfew. Ava lost count of the number of times he'd sworn how he would never forgive himself if something happened to her. He always took blame for everything Brianna did. It hurt Ava knowing that Brianna never cared about how much worry she caused him. Even though DeWayne, no matter what, loved them and always supported them.

"Uncle, I hope you didn't believe—"

"Not for a second. That's why I did nothing. I told them I wouldn't sign and that I'd handle you myself. It was all I could say to give me time to think. I've been busy with a lot of tests."

"I'm so sorry to worry you like this, Uncle."

"You don't worry about that. I'm doing fine."

"What do I do, then? Should I call the police and—"

"No. I've already spoken with my lawyers. I wanted to talk to you first before making any final decisions. I'll take care of it. When we get off the phone, I'll call my lawyers back. Promise me, whatever you do, don't let Brianna know you and I have spoken, do you hear me? And I want you to take a picture of the papers with your phone and send them to my lawyers, *Brown and Brown*. You'll find their information in my Rolodex on my desk."

"Yes, sir," she said, already flipping through it. "Found it."

"Good. Ava, please be careful and get to safety before the storm comes," DeWayne added with great concern in his voice.

"I will. I have everything under control. After I get done here, I'm coming to the hospital to be with you, okay?"

"Okay."

"I love you," Ava said fondly.

"I love you too. Everything will be fine, I promise."

Ava ended the call, dropped her cell back into her purse and looked up to find Brianna standing in the doorway.

Chapter Seventeen

"There they are. I've been looking all over for those." Brianna walked in and slammed the door shut behind her.

"You won't get away with this, Brie," Ava said, turning the key, quickly locking the documents inside the drawer. Her heart raced with fear. If her sister did all this behind her back, what else is she capable of?

"Shocked, you're not the only one with brains around here, huh?" Brianna smirked. "Don't you want to know how I got Uncle's signature? That's the best part."

"Brianna, please…" Ava said nervously.

"Remember when you gave me the keys to Uncle's office, so I could get the petty cash? You ended up being such a trooper. You gave me the ammunition I needed, the key to Uncle's office. I, of course, apologized for not bringing your keys back until way later in the evening, but well…you know, it takes time to run and get a copy made. You gave me full access to any and all kinds of documents with good ole' Uncle's signature. I almost succeeded a while back, the day you fainted and Paul had to carry your poor little ole' self to the cot? I stole your set of keys you left in the laundry room when you went to make those damn muffins. However, I guess you remembered leaving them in there, because as soon as I got the door unlocked, I heard your footsteps, so I returned the keys where I'd found them. Although I must say, it would be easier if you'd just tell me where you hide the other sets. No worries, though. I knew another time would present itself, and it did."

Ava gripped the arms of her chair and thought back. After she fainted and Paul carried her to the cot in DeWayne's office, she knew she'd locked his door and didn't know how Paul could have gotten in. Now it all made sense. Ava felt sick to her stomach. "I can't believe you'd do this. To Uncle

DeWayne of all people, the only one who took us in after mom and dad died," Ava said sadly.

"That's in the past girl, get over it. I have!" Brianna spat in anger.

"Why—why are you doing this?" Ava asked, getting up from the chair. She walked around the desk and stood with her back to the window as she faced Brianna and the door. Brianna blocked the only way out, and for the first time in her life, she feared her sister.

"You know why! You can't have Paul…" Brianna fumed, waving her hand out in front of her. "…And all this too. Do you think DeWayne will turn this over to me one day? No. It will be you…Miss Perfect. Well, I'll see to it that I get what I deserve. No matter what!"

"You did all this because of Paul?" Ava asked. "You went to Uncle DeWayne and tried to force him to sign those papers just because of jealously?"

Brianna sneered, "Paul's not the only reason. Like I said, I deserve more." She paced around the room, a sly smile spreading across her face. "And it wasn't just me, Marc went with me that day at the hospital. After I told him about Uncle DeWayne's money, he helped come up with the plan and how we could leave this godforsaken place. Marc is right Ava, Uncle owes me."

"Brianna, it's over. Uncle DeWayne knows what you tried to do." Ava shook her head. "He'll never give you what you want. Not this way."

At the same time, the sound of booming winds indicated they were running out of time.

Ava took a few steps closer to her sister when the window behind her exploded. Glass struck her in the head and lower back. She winced from the pain and fell to her knees. Her hand instantly went to the wound.

"I'll still get what's mine!" Brianna yelled, as she ran over to the desk while Ava still lay on the floor, took her keys and opened the drawer. She pulled out the checkbook, ripped out a handful of blank checks, and stuffed them inside her purse.

"Brie, don't," Ava said, panting in pain.

Brie rushed back to the door, reached inside her purse and unexpectedly, pulled out a gun. "Don't what, huh?" she said, aiming a gun directly at Ava. "You've been telling me what to do for far too long, sis. It's time I took charge."

"No, don't do this. This isn't you, Brie!" Ava cried.

"I told you. I'm doing what I must. Now, stay back or I'll shoot."

"No, you won't. You couldn't shoot your own sister. I love you, Brie."

Objects started to lift and fly around the room from the monstrous storm as it attacked through the shattered window. Papers, office supplies, pictures on the walls flew across the room.

Something smacked Ava in the back of her head again. Another piece of glass? Her hand immediately went to the injury and discovered more blood. "Brianna, please." Ava slowly got to her feet. Unbalanced, she still progressed closer to her.

"Stop. I swear I'll shoot!" Brianna hollered.

"No…No you won't. I—" Light-headed, Ava continued one small step after the other, trying her best to hold herself upright. She was only able to take a couple steps toward Brianna. "I love you, Brie. You and DeWayne are all I have left," Ava wept, then even with everything she had, she couldn't stand any longer and fell to the floor. Her hand went to the back of her head and felt the blood still gushing from the earlier blow. Slowly the barrel of the gun started to lower. A sigh of relief flooded her. "Help me, Brie. Help me."

Brianna rushed over to Ava, tears streaming down her face. "Ava, I'm—I'm so sorry. Seeing you like this, bleeding all over the place, I can't—I could never hurt you." She cried and squeezed Ava.

"It's okay...we've got to get to safety. I need your help. Where's Paul?" Ava wouldn't make it by herself. The increase of blood loss made her queasy.

"Sure, hang on. I think Paul's working on boarding up the units. I'll go find him." Brianna rushed across the hall to the laundry room and came back with a towel in hand. She placed it at the back of Ava's head to help stop the blood.

Then a man walked in right behind her. "What the hell! Why is she still alive?"

Brianna turned and placed her palm on the guy's chest, stopping him from advancing.

"Marc, wait. We can't do this. She's my sister!"

"What? I knew you'd go soft. This was your plan and we *will* finish it, Brianna. You promised me money."

"No—no, you don't understand. I changed my mind. I can't shoot my own sister," Brianna argued.

"Well…" He pushed Brianna aside. "If you can't do it…I will. She knows too much. Next, we'll go pay your uncle a visit. We should've killed that bastard in the first place."

Then everything happened in slow motion. Even the high winds seemed calm. A loud bang rang across the room. Did he actually pull the trigger? Ava pushed herself halfway up using her elbow, lifting her head from the glass and debris-covered floor. Her other hand instantly went to the wound at her abdomen. She touched it then spread her fingers out in front of her, gasping at the sight of blood. The pain at her stomach intensified as she gazed over at Brianna.

Brianna, covered her mouth with her hands in shock as tears ran down her cheeks. She ran over to Marc and pounded on his chest, screaming, "You killed her! You killed her!"

Seconds later, Ava's body jerked at the sound of a second shot. This time, she knew the bullet hadn't hit her. Closing her eyes, Ava prayed to awaken from this nightmare, but upon opening them again and blinking several times, she focused in on the body lying in front of her.

Brianna.

Marc was gone.

Ava's breathing lessened and her gasps of breath became difficult. Brianna's body lay motionless a couple feet away. Tears swelled in Ava's eyes. She tried lifting her body, but strangely, her own weight was too much to bear. She collapsed onto the carpet and wept, realizing they'd been left there to die.

Chapter Eighteen

Finished boarding the east side units, Percival started in on the west side when a loud bang came from out of nowhere. The second he heard the shot, a strange darkness pulled at his soul.

AVA!

His boots beat through the wet sand. The high winds were nothing for him. He flew through the heavy storm and without using his hands, burst open the doors to the office building. Searching the kitchen then behind the front counter, he turned and darted his attention down the hall leading to DeWayne's office. He stopped in his tracks when he reached the doorway. Even as an angel Percival couldn't have prepared

himself for what he saw—both Ava and
Brianna shot, blood seeping from their
bodies and forming pools as they lie on the
floor.

Instantly, he rushed over to Ava and
waved his hands frantically over her body,
not knowing where he needed to attend to
first.

Faint sounds came from Ava. "Brie—
help—Brie."

"No, Ava, you are dying. Let me help
you, please. Oh God, please?" He begged.

"No. Sister. First," she muttered, even
more winded than seconds before.

Percival gritted his teeth, but got up and
went over to Brianna. It didn't register until
he gazed down at her.

Dead. Mission. Failed.

No. No—you can't be! Percival thought
remorsefully.

The sound of Ava coughing spurred
Percival to rush back over to her. With his
powers, he scanned inside her body and fear
nearly froze him as death began to take hold
of her. With his mission on Earth failed,
what Percival did next, he did without a
second thought. Carefully lifting Ava, he

carried her into the main area of the building. He needed space. Delicately placing her on the wooden flooring, he ripped his T-shirt free, willed his wings to appear and expanded their seven-foot length behind him. His wings were only half covered with feathers. They looked so frail and thin. It was only a matter of time before he would be stripped of them altogether. So, he didn't have time to waste.

Percival knelt on both knees, placing his hand over Ava's heart and called forth his powers. All at once, an incandescent glow emitted from his frame, followed by his wings coming around to cover them both like a tight sleeve. Securely surrounded, he reached deeper, summoning all the power in his being. A glow extended from his wings. It grew brighter and brighter with each passing second. Creating a miracle, he sought out the bullet wedged deep inside her tiny frame. Slowly drawing it from within the skin and tissues, he carefully removed it altogether from her abdominal region. Finally, he worked on healing the damaged internal organs, then sealed the wound. Next, he sealed the cuts on her head and back. Double-checking the rhythm of her heart as it slowly steadied itself, he listened to her breathing, not stopping until she'd been completely healed.

Offering Ava his energy and full strength of his spirit, he willed her all that remained in him, for she was his life, no matter the sacrifice.

With heavy eyelids, Ava blinked and tried to focus on her surroundings. An unfamiliar setting caused her to sit up in a hurry.

"Have no fear. You are safe," a familiar voice said.

"Paul? Is that you? Where are you? Where am I? What happened? Where's Brianna?"

Examining the area, it dawned on her now, how she sat in some kind of parking garage. Concrete walls from as far as the eye could see. Matching columns and hundreds of lines marking parking spaces surrounded her. The only light came from floodlights positioned on every other column. The howling winds around her, reminded her hurricane Ben still raged outside.

Gradually, a shadow emerged at her left, then Paul's frame came into view—but it wasn't Paul. His face and body matched, but wait—were those wings behind him? She had to take a second look. If those were wings, what happened to his feathers? They didn't even stand tall behind him, only dragged in back of him as he walked toward her. "Paul?"

His head lowered as he drew nearer. "Yes. That is the name I go by on Earth, but my spiritual name is Percival."

"Percival? Who—what are you? What's going on? Where's Brianna?"

"I am an angel. Sent on a mission to save your sister's soul, yet I failed. I am so sorry, Ava. Brianna is dead. I could not save her."

Ava plopped back down on the concrete floor.

"I am so sorry. I tried. You asked me to save her first and I tried, but she was already dead. I have no power over the dead. But, you were dying too, so I—I saved you."

Ava gazed down at her stomach and pulled up her shirt. Nothing. No wounds anywhere to show she'd been shot. "I don't understand...You're a—?"

"I am an angel of God, Ava. And my time here is done. I must go. I wanted you to know even though you will not remember me after I am gone."

"Now, wait a minute." Ava slowly stood up. "I don't believe this. Angels. My sister. You healing me—does this sound crazy to you? Are you serious? What the hell is going on?"

"I know it is hard to understand. But believe me, what I say is true. I needed you to hear it from my own lips before I go." Percival sighed.

"This is too much. I can't..." Ava became light-headed. Everything around her swayed and she blinked, fighting to stay alert.

Percival leaned in, lightly pressing his lips against hers. A happiness shone on his face and his skin even glowed with it.

Ava felt an energy jolting through her body, she felt love swell in her chest and mind. A pure electric feeling of joy, like she'd never known.

Drawing back, Percival quietly whispered in her ear.

Ava tried to discern what he whispered, but she couldn't seem to grasp it, then she passed out in his arms.

Chapter Nineteen

Out in the moonlight, Ava stood at the end of the catwalk and stared at the tide rushing in, crashing against her ankles. Only a sliver of the sun remained before it sank into the ocean. Whenever she went to the place where she and Percival stood that first day after he arrived, she always felt at peace. A magical spot where she'd fallen in love for the first time in her life.

Ava recalled the night Percival saved her, a time in her life she would never forget. Paul and Percival, the angel, were one in the same. It became obvious to her now, once she thought about it. With each time he'd been near, he always made her believe everything would be okay.

A month had passed since that terrible day. After she'd been shot and Percival took her to the parking garage at the hospital, the same one holding her uncle. He told her about himself then. Then after blacking out, she finally came to, and called out for Percival, but he never appeared. Feeling a deep sadness, she got up and took an elevator up into the hospital to see her uncle. She thought about all that happened, letting everything sink in. Ava still found it hard to believe.

To this day, she never spoke about Percival to anyone. She would only mention the time when a man named Paul helped her around the condo while her uncle was ill. God Himself must have sent Paul to her, even though he said his mission was for her sister. That's what got her through each day. Anyone else, she thought might not have dealt with everything so calmly. The more she recalled the times she had with Percival, the more she felt blessed to know him and thanked God for sending such miracles down to people such as her and her sister. She never would have made it without his help and would forever be grateful. When DeWayne inquired about what had happened to her handyman, Ava told him

Paul had been called back home. In a way it was the truth. DeWayne simply said it'd been a pity he didn't get to thank him.

The hurricane passed too, leaving behind only minor damage. A few broken windows that hadn't been boarded up, lots of leaves from surrounding trees and other debris was all she'd found. For the most part, the resort hadn't been hit as hard as predicted. Sadly, Brianna's partner, Marc did more damage to the place than the hurricane.

DeWayne also recovered, although he still seemed weak. It would be a little longer before he could come back to work full-time, but he did return home. He insisted he could take care of the accounting books for the business, which didn't require a lot of energy. Ava had a hard time trying to talk him out of it. So, while not being able to hold back at his persistence, she'd given in. The doctor said a little exercise would be good, so each day with Ava's help, DeWayne walked from his condo unit to the office. Ava made sure he didn't stay longer than a few hours.

A few days after the murder of her sister, Ava learned the police received a call with a tip that Marc had been spotted. They arrested him on sight a few hours later. After the evidence verified Ava's testimony, the state prosecutor intended to go to trial and asking for the death penalty. Marc ended up changing his plea to guilty for a lesser sentence. But would remain behind bars for a long while.

Ava slept well at night knowing the judge awarded him life in prison without parole. Her statement included Marc manipulated Brianna into drawing up those papers. He'd forged the documents with their uncle's signature, so they could get money and run off together.

In spite of Brianna's wicked ways and deceit at plotting against her uncle, and even though Brianna was responsible for what happened to her, Ava still missed her sister. Now it was only her and DeWayne.

Ava survived and kept sane by clinging tightly to her memories of Percival. The last memory of him, when he revealed his true form, at first haunted her for many nights. Then over time, she accepted and believed angels did exist and walked among them.

It was a comforting feeling.

Over the passing months though, one thing bothered Ava. She hoped Brianna's soul passed into peace in Heaven, but sadly, she'd never know. With everything that happened, Ava made sure never to take life for granted. Life, a precious gift, should be cherished. One never knew their expiration date, only God knew ones ending.

A cool breeze from nowhere brushed across Ava's skin and goose bumps rose along her arms. She smiled as she looked at the bumps on her arm. It was a kiss from Percival. Before he left, he whispered in her ear about how when she felt a soft evening breeze, it would be him sending his love to her. Oh, how she pined for him.

Pressing both palms over her heart, she closed her eyes and with a broken whisper, cried out to him. "Why do you still haunt me? Can't you see what you're doing? Your presence lingers and—and I can't stand knowing you'll never take me in your arms. You said I'd never remember you. Well, I do. I love you, do you hear me?" Ava dropped to her knees. When her shins hit the wood, she felt the sting of impact but ignored it. They were the very planks

Percival replaced with his own bare hands. She leaned forward, placing her palms on the catwalk and peered up at the deep-purple sky. "Help me. Help me, please, Percival. Take away all this pain. I can't live another day. You gave me a glimpse into Heaven and then took it all away."

She again remembered how on the day he told her what he truly was, something seemed different in his appearance. Books always foretold that angels wielded the most beautiful and magnificent wings one could imagine. However, when Percival stood before her in the garage, his were not. There were bare spots among his set of wings. Like a dog with mange, large sections of feathers were missing from each wing. They also appeared thin and frail. For weeks, she replayed it over and over in her mind. She couldn't help but feel she had something to do with it. If he sacrificed himself for her, she could never forgive herself. Was he alive? Did he die to save her? Is that why he had to leave? Tortured thoughts consumed and ate at her soul. So many unanswered questions would probably haunt her forever.

There on the catwalk, Ava cried out into the night, her hands covering her face. Her tears fell over the tops of her fingers and then onto to the planks of wood below.

Chapter Twenty

$\mathcal{G}$azing down into an endless array of clouds, Percival watched Ava from the heavens. For weeks, each pain-inflicted word she uttered tore at his soul. He kept watching Ava through a portal and ached at not being able to give her comfort. It saddened him to the fact there only seemed to be one solution left. This time, he couldn't fail. He must strip all memories she possessed of him while on Earth. He couldn't allow her to spend the rest of her life in such grief and blame herself for his actions. He thought he'd erased her memories of him before this. The night she'd been shot, he entered her mind to instill his influence and replace all memories of him. Humans couldn't handle something like this, he knew that. Though, before he erased all memory of him, he could fight his love for her no longer and kissed her passionately.

How did he fail in removing her memory of him? As much as it tortured him, he knew what he needed to do. Angels never fell in love with mortals and because he had, he faced the aftermath. This sacrifice would be harder than anything. It made him recall the horrible night Brianna had been killed and he'd been summoned back to Heaven.

With Brianna dead, and having failed his mission, only a few feathers remained on his wings now. Percival knew it wouldn't be long until they were stripped from him altogether.

"What are you doing, my son?" The voice of God spoke from behind him.

Percival knew he should not be using the portal this way. He turned toward God and remaining silent, he bowed reverently. Nothing he could utter would be new to God's ears. The Lord knew all. He'd failed and Brianna's soul had most likely gone to Sheol. When he bent forward, the exposed bare bones of what use to be his wings hung lifeless behind him. "I could not save her. I am so sorry, my Lord." Percival dropped to his knees and inclined his head down with shame.

"Are you so sure her soul is lost?" God asked.

"My Lord?" Percival peered up just as God turned around and waved his arm out in front of him.

Clouds parted and an image off in the distance started to take shape. A woman's face…a white robe…blonde hair blowing freely behind her.

"No. No. It cannot—" Percival got to his feet and took a few steps forward, but stopped in shock.

There stood Brianna. "Percival, I'm sorry I've been so difficult. The sad part is, it came too late and I never told Ava how much I really loved her. Truly, I did. Everything is so clear up here. I don't expect her to ever forgive me, but will you make sure she knows I'm truly sorry and how much I love her?"

It stunned him to discover he didn't fail after all, and at the same time, Percival's back started to prickle. Suddenly, he glanced behind him. His set of wings stretched far out, strong, full and magnificent. He smiled excitedly and flapped them in pleasure.

"You did not fail, my son. Even at one's last moments in life, their soul can be saved and Brianna chose the right path. Her soul will now rest within Heaven's realm, forever," God declared.

Percival beamed with happiness, but turning back to Brianna, he frowned because he wouldn't be able to fulfill her request. "I am sorry. I will not be able to grant your wish. You see, I shall never see Ava again," Percival said sadly. It pained him to see the look on Brianna's face when she knew her sister would never know how much she loved her. Although in truth, what hurt more was *he* would never see Ava again. With everything he almost sacrificed, he still loved Ava. Except now, she suffered and yearned for him. She needed to move on with her life. Memories of him would only prevent her from doing so.

Brianna nodded silently and turned away to move back into the clouds.

"I ask again, why do you continually concern yourself with this human, Percival? Your mission is over, is it not?" God spoke.

"Forgive me, my Lord." Percival bowed in respect.

"You know it is forbidden to have contact with humans once your assignment is done. Brianna is among us. Why do you watch the remaining sibling?"

"She is…" Percival gazed humbly at his Lord and Savior. "She is suffering. I feel her pain. I do not know why, yet it consumes me with every passing second. I think of nothing else while she walks upon earth in such turmoil. It's because of me, Lord. I did this to her."

"Yes. I know, my son." With a wave of his hand, God reopened the portal. There, while peering down, it remained clear Ava still wept. The sun had set behind the ocean. Alone, she sat surrounded by dark shadows with only a soft radiance of moonlight reflecting off the waters. "Hear me, my child…" God turned and stared at Percival. A loving warm glow exuded around His entire body. "…Do you know why you are able to sense the human's emotions? This has happened to only one before now. An Archangel. The Archangels remain in Heaven, although you shall not see nor converse with them. As you are already aware, their fate is already decided. Yours I feel has a different path."

Percival stood absolutely still, wondering what His Lord meant to do now.

God placed his hand upon Percival's shoulder. "My son, when you saved Ava from the afterlife, a part of your soul united with hers. It will forever be connected. This is why even in Heaven, you are able to sense the human's emotions."

"What do you mean?" Percival asked, perplexed.

"Only the rarest spirit and one of purest faith may be connected with an angel's soul. You are ordained to be together. Thus, is the reason you were drawn to her on Earth. It is rare for one of my own creation to share this kind of connection. But I shall not deny two souls fated for one another."

Percival hung his head. "But I am…immortal. She is not."

A strange sensation of warmth overcame him. A feeling of—*hope and—love*.

"A chance at life shall I give to you. Most do not receive such an offering. Use this time well. I shall see you both again."

Enthralled by such graciousness, Percival became speechless, bowed again to his Lord and Savior, then kneeled, kissing the bottom of His holy robe. "Forgive me, my Lord. But may I ask for—?"

"You need not ask, my son. Brianna will know you have delivered the message she so desired from you."

A great wave of gratitude spread through Percival's being, then suddenly everything faded. Seconds passed and like a fog lifting, things around him began to take their form. He had to blink more than once. The most glorious thing he thought to ever see glimmered from only a few feet away.

Ava.

Percival drew in the fresh, salty sea air, his first as a human. It smelled like rain, sand, water, life, love—oh, he could go on. He scanned his body and it felt strange not to have wings. His upper torso was bare, yet white cotton pants hung around his lower frame. Barefoot, he ambled toward Ava. "Do not cry, my love," he called out softly from behind her.

Ava's whimpers ceased and slowly she turned. Getting to her feet, she didn't move from where she stood. Wiping tears from her eyes, she blinked several times. "No. It can't be."

Percival stepped closer, then captured her cheek in his palm. "I shall never leave your side again," he said, wiping her lingering tears away with his thumb.

A grin spread across Ava's lips. Instantly, her arms flew around his neck and she kissed him with everything she had.

He returned the embrace, picking her up and swinging her around in their joyous reunion. The rest of his mortal life, blessed by the grace of God, would be spent loving this woman.

Finally, placing Ava down, his heart beat rapidly for the first time with thankfulness and overwhelming human emotion. He raised her chin with one finger and kissed the tip of her nose. Then lowered his forehead placing it gently on hers and vowed, "I will always love you. Never, will you feel pain or sorrow. Love shall surround you and your family...from now until the time we reunite in the heavens and live amongst the angels."

Ava smiled, placing her palm over Percival's heart. "I love you, my guardian angel. And when the time comes when we reach the heavens, I will thank the Lord who sent you back to me. To Him, I will forever be grateful."

Percival smiled with such devotion and affection for Ava's admiration of God. He took her by the hand and they headed toward the condos.

"What happened to your wings?" Ava asked as they walked hand-in-hand.

Percival glanced over at Ava's worrisome expression. Oh, how he loved this woman. He stopped and took her by the shoulders. "My love, I am human. I am no longer immortal or an angel of God. See?" He turned around and the single feather signifying the mark of God was no longer branded upon his skin. "I do not bear the mark of an angel of God. I am to remain on Earth to love you and even though I am not an angel, I shall protect your soul and look after you for all eternity."

Ava smiled and threw her arms around him.

Percival placed a kiss upon her forehead. "Oh, and I have a message from one dear to you…" Percival swallowed hard. He hoped the news didn't bring on more pain. "…Brianna. She said to tell you she loves you and always has."

A tear slid down from the corner of her eye. She didn't say a word, just nodded.

Percival knew nothing more needed said. He took Ava's hand in his, lifting it to his mouth to gently kiss the inside of her palm. "Come. I'd like to meet this uncle of yours."

"I know he'd like to meet you too." Ava grinned.

As they walked, he took a moment to gaze up at the stars.

A voice spoke around them. "Love her. Cherish her. This is my gift to you. You will live a happy and wondrous life together, Percival. I bless thee with all that I am."

"Thank you," Percival whispered.

"What did you say?" Ava asked with a puzzled look on her face.

"Nothing my love, let's go." Percival smiled and wrapped an arm around Ava, as they headed up toward DeWayne's condo.

To start a new life…*together.*

The miracle given to him by God. One where he would make sure both Ava and her uncle lived surrounded by love and happiness.

About the Author

Scarlet Hunter by day, works full time as a Director for a TPA (Third Party Administrator) company for Section 125 benefit plans. Residing in the outskirts of Memphis, Tennessee, when not working at her full-time job, she is found typing away on her laptop. Scarlet released her first self-publication in February 2013. As an avid reader, Scarlet's love of science-fiction/paranormal romances inspired her to pursue her dream of writing. You can visit her website to find all the great stuff in the works.

OTHER BOOKS
BY
SCARLET HUNTER

Thirst of the Sea

Dust of Darkness, Book One,
The Reign of Darkness

Curator's Curse, Book One
Legends of the Immortal Bloods

Coming in 2014

Burning Salvation

Coming in 2015

Snowline's Visitor, Book One,
Arise of the Guardians

Mid-Night Mountain, Book Two,
Arise of the Guardians

Demon's Light, Book Two,
The Reign of Darkness